TALES OF THE BOOKSHELVES

DANCE WITH ME

LIVIA J. ELLIOT

Cover by Livia J. Elliot.

Artwork by José Arturo Bustamante

Artwork rights: Fernando Gamboa

Edited by Fernando Gamboa

Interior design and formatting by Livia J. Elliot.

ISBN 978-1-76354-386-7 (ebook)

ISBN 978-1-7635438-3-6 (paperback)

ISBN 978-1-7635438-4-3 (hardback)

ISBN 978-1-7635438-5-0 (audiobook)

A copy of this book is held by the National Library in Canberra under the legal deposit provisions of the Copyright Act 1968.

To Fernando.
For his courage and loving patience
while dancing with me.

CONTENTS

A note on the English language

Before you read, please note that my **flavour** of English is Australian. I **apologise** to everyone in advance. Please don't be concerned if you **realise** something is wrong, or think I've committed an **offence**. Who knows, you may even get used to it while **travelling** through the pages.

"Oh, no!" You may exclaim, but rest assured, the quotes remain double.

Also, shall you encounter ~~strike through text~~, know that it is intended. Due to its origins as a book-with-choices, 'Dance With Me' leverages some ergodic elements. I hope you find them interesting.

That said, I'm **honoured** that you are interested in my work, and hope you'll enjoy it.

~Livia, a writer with Aussie grammar.

Regarding Content Warnings

This is a story about depression and emotional trauma, told through a number of allegories.

'*Dance With Me*' discusses sadness, apathy, mourning, resilience, undeserved abuse, self-worth, and hiding in loneliness. Quietly, it discusses preconceptions and how they can change as life changes us. It touches on the difficulties of trusting a good, honest partner and having one's world view shattered by events we cannot control.

It is not an easy story to read, but the ending is positive. Nevertheless, reader's discretion is advised.

Depression lurks near all of us, so seek help if you need it and, whatever you do, stay safe.

A Beautiful World

The magic awakens me, bringing the colours of life, sparkling golden and opalescent. The scent is overwhelming, a sweet but earthy fragrance, like silk and oil paintings, thickening the air into a soothing welcome. I breathe, but the stiff ceramic of my body barely moves, the air's perfume whiffing away rather than blending in.

The enchantment fades but the music teases me sluggishly, falling into a sequence only to shy away. I feel it chiming on my fingertips, tinkling on my ceramic toes... yet it slacks again, threatening with oblivion.

A mechanism creaks, a winding key twirls around, and the music gives me life.

It flows unrestrained through my ceramic body, blossoming into reality. I flourish in a coil of elegance, rounding with an arm poised up, my wrist tilting, fingers spread. I kneel, and my romantic tutu flows like delicate petals edged in gold, spiralling alongside me, bobbling while I pirouette, whirling with the music.

The ballet is my purpose and joy, and I drift with the tune. Each note revives me, each sequence reinforcing the magic. I giggle and someone echoes my bliss, delighted.

I keep dancing, uncaring about my surroundings. Their bliss joins the melody, each gasp adding chimes, each giggle strengthening the spell that binds and enlivens me. I leap and pirouette, uncaring about where the dance floor is—this music just brought me alive, and dancing is essential to my existence; it *is* me.

Another jubilant gasp whooshes by and only then I look around. An elven boy stands nearby, clasping his walnut hands below his belt. His neck and head are partly shadowed by the shelf above, a halo of light surrounding his body as it eclipses the room's chandelier. He moves slightly and I notice the intricately braided hair, his opulent lips gasping with bewilderment, and his emerald doe-eyes.

I smile back from my music box, and the boy's joy ignites my magic. The melody decants and I adage, a forefinger reaching towards him. He leans slowly, captivated and trying to touch my miniature finger.

With a brisé, I waltz playfully sideways, catching his attention. He watches me as I swivel, following the melody around the dance floor.

A crescendo livens up the magic and I glide through the music box's narrow area, tracing its circular, gilded edge but returning to the centre. I fouetté, over and over, spinning and whipping my leg in perfect synchrony with the melody all around me. My gentleness catches his gaze, drawing a gasp and sparkling giggles.

The tune halts as I salute with both arms up, and the elven boy claps again, skipping in place. His gigantic height becomes comprehensible, and vertigo overwhelms me—he is so disproportionately large that the barest of movements could damage me irreparably. A shiver of dread tickles my smooth ceramic shoulders, yet I stand regally, holding a lovely smile. Charmed by my acting, the boy bends with arms stretched down, but the edge of the shelf's floor and ceiling hide part of the movement.

"Such a charming figurine!" He says with a smile, head so

large it covers my entire field of view. "I'll name you Lyra because of the music you dance to."

"How should I call you?" I ask as gentle as possible, curtseying—but although my mouth shapes the words, no sound reverberates past me. Bewilderment floods me as the silence stretches until I finally understand.

He can't hear me because his magic didn't grant me a voice. It gave me purpose and let me dance... but that is all it did.

My ugly silence does not linger, soon livened by the boy's amused chuckling. He backtracks, stretching his arms towards the shelf as if to command it. Wood creaks and glass clatters on a frame, and two large doors loom in front of me, embracing the cupboard to seal me within it. A latch—hidden from my view— clicks locked somewhere, and the sounds beyond the glass mute down.

The elven boy casts his gaze above and below my level, hands clasped at his back. He takes a few more steps away and nods with pride before turning and departing; his embroidered long jacket flares artfully with each step, almost casting a rhythm I cannot forget.

I follow him with my gaze towards the room's thick wooden door, my heart sinking the closer he gets to it. At last it creaks open and the boy vanishes, shutting it behind him. Another latch clicks locked, sealing the doorframe motionless, golden light rimming its edges.

A clock ticks endlessly as I remain centred on the dancing area, waiting for his next command—but nothing happens. Half an hour later, I finally sigh, releasing my posture.

My gaze decants to my pointe flats while curiosity overwhelms me. I haven't seen myself, so eager I was to dance for the boy—and so I lift my hands to watch the pale, bisque ceramic. My fingers are slender, and my palms are smooth, flexing without marking the material. Bending, I touch the textureless romantic tutu sculpted in ceramic and awakened by magic. It has a peplum of gilded petals, baring my collarbone, hugging my lithe ballerina body, and barely grazing my knees. My legs are strong but svelte, and my pointe shoes lace up through my calves, unremovable.

Movement distracts me, and my reflection in the glass doors catches my attention. I have a cinnamon updo, blushed pale cheeks, and tawny eyes. A roguish smile curls my lips—faintly tinted in a demure pink—but my gaze scatters into the background, following the shimmers of light on the circular, gilded edge of the dancing area.

I amble through its glazed mirror surface, each step dainty and measured, toes first before gently pressing the heel down. The music box's lid opens at the back, trimmed in gold filigree and brimming with the magic that mists the edges. It feels small, but I pirouette into a corner and collect my breath before performing a grand jeté all across; I bow upon landing, clapping in delight—my box is nicely sized.

The contentment lasts very little, as another detail captures my incessant curiosity—I haven't seen much of this cupboard, and this shelf extends tantalisingly.

Mindful of my steps, I approach the gilded edge of the music box and peer down. The shelf's lacquered wooden ground seems distant, reflecting the scattered gemstones that emanate a magical, colourful mist. Stretching, I see a silver-carved tiara, miniature portraits, and a book holder restraining leather-bound books.

Curiosity sparks me into a nervous titter, and I shyly stretch my leg out of the music box, hoping to descend—yet my pointe shoes grace the sculpted shore, the toes teasing the air itself. Another shiver tickles my ceramic shoulders and I pull back, heart battering and unhinged. Scared, I attempt to sit on the box's cliff, but vertigo forces me to retreat further inside, clutching my rampaging chest.

The dread of falling paralyses me and I glance around, not

daring to move much more; after all, the elven boy may return soon and I should be ready to dance for him whenever he arrives. A penumbra shades the gigantic room, but after blinking, I see the contours of the opulent furniture taking most of the space.

The table at the room's centre is round, walnut-made and lacquered, decorated with pressed flowers as a mantelpiece. A single chair of impressive manufacture crowns the narrower side, a small filigree toolbox near it. Beyond them, I notice the other cabinets lining the walls—and I take time to study them from my vantage point. The bookcase at my right sparkles golden as if lanterns flickered from its books, and those cupboards across the room seem to absorb the light that permeates through the curtained window; they appear... old and unkempt, their contents sealed behind thick wooden doors.

I stare at them for a long moment, my fingers grazing my lips as I wonder whatever they may hold. That unsettling curiosity overwhelms me again, and I peer down at the music box's edge —then gasp in realisation. The shelf's wooden floor is an inch away from the closed glass door, leaving enough space for me to slide down into my demise.

Apprehension tightens my shoulders for a long pause, my heart skipping a beat or two—until voices and merriment seep from that gap. It quells my incipient weariness and, only after a few tempos, light suffuses into my level.

A smile curls my lips, soothing yet gentle. Clearly, there are more enchanted figurines in this room.

That realisation ignites my inquisitiveness, and I kneel with my hands on the dance floor's mirrored surface, my slender body stretching to peer down. I glimpse right and left, eagerness building up as I seek something with relentless desire. My motions are always elegant, proper of a ballerina like me... yet they slow down, stalled by confusion.

What am I looking for? Why would I attempt to leave this music box?

The answers elude me, impossible and unreal and so I stare at the room beyond in search for clues—the dark cupboard across the room, the table's mantlepiece, and the abyssal gap before the glass doors. The latter induces giddiness, startling me out of my reverie and terrorising me with a fall.

I blink it away, but the peril persists like an endless refrain, sustained and resonant albeit unwanted. It fades slowly, carried away by the constant ticking of a clock I cannot see, its echoes subdued by the voices of the statuettes inhabiting the other shelves.

My eyes close as I keen into that music so natural and loving. I can hear movement, fabric shushing, pages turning, and melodies arising from everywhere around me... and imagine the beautiful silhouettes, some wooden-made, others porcelain, some elongated and delicate, others smooth and elegant. I open my eyes to seek them, following the flickering dots of miniature candles on the other cupboards and shelves. My lips press into a prim smile, a gentle chuckle escaping me as I note the steps traversing the ledge above me.

There is a world in this room, so full of life and magic, of beauty and art.

I stand again, eager to be part of it until a yawn overtakes me. Sleep demands my attention and I do not refuse it—I must rest to wake up and dance for the boy when he comes to see me.

Prodding my elaborate updo, I assess my music box from my position; beautifully made, gilded and flourished, gentle yet opulent. A velvet sleeping bed awaits near the open lid, and I tiptoe towards it, dainty and flowing like a proper ballerina. Kneeling close by, I graze the mauve, soft fabric with my fingertips before sliding inside. It is snug, securing my body between cushions.

Relaxing, I hum a quiet melody, letting the comfort drift me into a dreamless sleep.

My slumber recedes gently, easing me into the new days's warmth. I prop myself up, sitting among the bed's velvety cushions—and the sight enthrals me. Gold light seeps from the dawn-rimmed door, casting a haze of bronze from a window hidden between shelves. The sheer curtains flow towards the inside, shivering mellowly.

Stretching to vanish the remnants of sleep, I crawl into the dancing area and elongate. I must ready myself for the new day, to dance for the elven boy.

I relax my back, breathing in and out while peering at the room; it is *wealthy*, and every wooden piece is ornamented or sculpted. Imagining a suitable opulent melody, I sway my waist and stretch my legs—but a new realisation startles me into a soft relevé. The shelves' lights from last night have vanished, the voices have quieted, and the entire world within this room now seems to await, expectant, the boy's arrival.

That understanding encourages me, tickling my toes as I complete my stretches and settle into second position—my feet at hip distance and turned around, blending into a perfect line, arms stretched to the sides with my fingers falling gracefully.

Hours pass in idle wait, but my ceramic body endures it motionless. I crave the music, to dance and feel the scented air flowing through my dress. My mind teases me with the possibility of my melody blossoming from the box, and a wistful sigh escapes me... but I cannot start it alone; its key is twice my size and meant for elven-sized fingers.

A few tempos later, the door creaks open and a soft, warm light bathes the room. The merry footfalls of the boy hop through, followed by the refined cadence of a woman. My heart pounds with anticipation, drumming like the markers before an orchestra begins—and finally, *finally*, the boy points at me.

His emerald eyes gleam joyfully, his features brightening at my sight. He turns, watching his mother's face, curly braids swiping his back with every motion. They talk with smiles on their lips, their conversation silent to me yet renewing my eagerness. Eventually, he tugs her long bell sleeve and pulls her towards my shelf.

The cupboard door tumbles as he struggles, shaking the furniture and panicking my heart—but amidst my attempts to remain composed, the mother's delicate, manicured toffee fingers move the boy away. The doors' latch unlocks gently, and her azure, velvety dress covers my field of view. Her nails are glossy teal ovals, shining bright when she deftly catches the box's crank. It clings, winding up, reigniting the magic inside me and sparkling it alive.

I dance, then. The ballet frees me, and the tune tingles alongside the spells awakening my body. I sway, closing my eyes and swiping the air with a pirouette. The tune flows, teasing and tantalising as I chase my reflection on the dance area, pirouetting and becoming one with the music.

It slows down too soon and I lament that cue; I was alive while I danced, yet I swirl in tandem with the slowing melody. The mother is still looking at me, so I adage, grazing her forefinger with my hand in a final salute.

"You truly are beautiful," the elven woman says, leaning gracefully to assess me; her cobalt eyes are cold but gentle. "Do you l—?"

She turns to the boy and her words are lost to me, silence overwhelming as she closes the cupboard's glass doors before retreating elsewhere.

Anxious, I spend the morning in the same position, waiting for another moment of glorious ballet... but as the clock ticks high above and the light fades into a coppery afternoon, my hopes vanish mercilessly.

Eventually, the night sparks the room alive again, and the distant echo of voices and life forms a tune in my mind. I miss the music, yet the more I glance at the box's key, the more I understand how impossible it is to spin it on my own.

Downcast I clasp my hands and close my eyes, my hopes reawakening as an idea blossoms within me. I could sing and dance to my own song, private and gentle, never too loud not to upset others.

Straightening, I swirl courteously and bashful, seeking my melody. The lyrics are elusive and so I chase them, realising I haven't spoken since my prior, failed experiment upon arrival. My attempt is clumsy, embarrassingly so, the words avoiding me before any can form. I know and understand, but translating my feelings into a language is more difficult than a grand jeté.

A hum of disappointment and frustration escapes me, yet its unsuspecting melody sparkles an idea—I don't need *words*; humming would be enough!

Excited, I move around with my hands linked behind my back, feeling that music that has been teasing me. My first song begins softly, shy and embarrassed like me, but growing bolder with every tempo. Slowly, I begin dancing on the mirror's surface, weaving melodies with movement for hours on end.

It's midnight when I sit down, still humming my music. When sleep finally embraces me I can almost *feel* the words forming on my lips.

Another day begins and I awaken to it under the mantle of that song I uncovered last night. It was my own, but not enough, incomplete and mangled because I'm meant to dance and not to sing—and so I swirl onto the glass-made floor, preparing for the boy and his mother. They can unlock the music box, enliven the enchantment that keeps me alive, and let me flourish to my full extent.

Their joy is my purpose, and so I stretch with mindful consideration before settling into a fourth position—one foot in front of the other but apart, each turned away from my body's centre. I lift the left arm into a gentle curve, the other stretched out but stately.

The few hours pass in pounding anxiety, its rhythm erratic and nervous. It gallops through me, racing my heart with expectation and hope, eager to sway and whirl—but the morning's light vanishes into the eerie quietude of noon, barely interrupted by the wind ululating outside the room; musicless and dark, restless like myself.

A certainty settles, unwanted but impossible to ignore—my fourth position was not attractive enough; neither elegant nor interesting to bring forth the elves. Desperation shivers through my legs and I present a relevé, my hopes resurfacing as my mind wanders to the locked winding key.

Eventually, the afternoon fades, and a new night arises.

There is nothing within me, just the emptiness and rejection left by that idle day. My doubts blossom, and I settle onto the dance floor, reticent and listless.

The other cupboards brim alive, but the impossibility of visiting them reignites my inner despair, consuming a few hours until I dither into a stand. I miss the music dearly, and the memory of the night before—of that hummed tune, of that shy dance—encourage me to try again.

Audacious, I flirt with a melody while finding a cadence, crooning and whispering until my humming blossoms, reverberating in a contralto to climb across the scales—and I dance to my own melody. Two pirouettes and a few motions later, my words sprout and echo on the shelf.

"The sweetest... of s-scents, the g-gen-tlest of kis-ses..." They trail in the space, absorbed by the wood, bouncing on the glass. I giggle and try again. "F-flow with the... air, tiny b-balle-rina of feat...t-thers."

I gasp, delighted even when crafting a mispronounced, senseless song. It is my own, and I dance to it while visiting each inch of my music box. My intonation needs considerable practice, but as the night wanes and the dawn approaches, I'm left with the feeling that someone clapped at my poor attempts.

Another sunrise tints the room in golden, and just like before I begin to elongate. Carefully, I use the dance floor's mirror to ensure my ceramic looks polished before standing in the middle, resolute.

I shall *not* repeat yesterday's mistake. Today I'll be elegance embodied, enchanting and luring to catch the boy's attention.

Pensive yet resolved, I pas de bourrée around the box's area, balancing and flowing alongside my thoughts. With a coil, I settle into fifth position—my feet close together, one before the other and turned away. I bring both hands closer at the front as if my fingers wanted to touch but could not.

To my delight, the door creaks open and the boy dashes inside, braids tumbling behind like his embroidered emerald coat. I present my best image but he ignores me, reaching for the bookshelf beside my cupboard. Muttering a few magic words, he summons a stool, stands on it, and retrieves a book.

The day flows in surly anticipation; the light changing within the room, the clock ticking restlessly while I silently fret. Why didn't he come to me? Did I irk him already? Weren't my pirouettes pleasant? Perhaps I didn't leap high enough, or overdid the grand adage.

The boy reads, and I worry. He swipes a page, and I despair. The paper hushes and he titters while my ceramic body hides my uneasiness with my perfect stance.

In the afternoon, he floats the book into the bookcase before approaching the exit with a smile. I remain in fifth position, enduring motionless and precise, elegant and hopeful as the door creaks open, illuminating the room with dusk and hope—yet he leaves without glancing back.

When that door closes, shadows encompass my cupboard, loneliness aching in my heart.

My wait endures like a fermata, resilient yet fading, mournful and hopeless. As the dusk's purple glimmer fades into darkness, I let my gaze roam left and right, taking in the lights sparkling on my shelf. They seem oblivious to the boy's rejection, uncaring of his needs, and independent of the elves that brought us alive.

My lips seal at that thought, neither smiling nor pouting, nor gesturing alongside the cacophony of feelings lurking within me.

A voice, one among the many in this room, distracts me at last; it approaches from the side, soft-spoken and charming, sweaty and peachy. I keen my hearing, wondering who she is, imagining myself meeting this refined lady and easing my loneliness. She sounds stately, definitely proper, my interest peaking the more she talks.

Intrigue leads me towards the box's edge, and vertigo mingles with curiosity until I look at the shelf's wooden floor, weighing how far it is. I failed my prior attempt at descending, consumed by fear—but the more this woman speaks, the more I want to meet her.

Kneeling again, I spread both palms firmly against the edge, muster my courage, and lean forwards to peer down into the box's side. There is a small set of gilded ornaments I could use as steps, each polished and glimmering under the faint light. This serviceable staircase has no handles, and that realisation terrifies me enough to scamper back—falling and cracking would be my end.

In the distance, the voice chuckles again, melodious yet rumbling, oblivious to my hesitations.

I jolt in surprise, trying to scowl, but my face doesn't move. The sensation... is strange, and so I forego my attempts to descend to watch myself in the mirror's reflection. My brown eyes and perfect updo meet me in a neutral expression, and after a moment I will myself to scowl—but nothing happens.

Moments pass as I try again with the same result, wishing to frown, willing to do so and only managing that pleasant, neutral countenance. Bewildered, I test other gestures, pouting, grimacing, narrowing my eyes, gasping in anger or startling in fear—but they refuse to appear. All of them. I feel the emotions, the anxiety building within me, yet my face remains gently restful.

I test a few tendus just to relax myself, swirl in place and then smile—and my features finally react. My cheeks puff lovingly, my pink lips spreading flirty yet coy, eyes arched with care and gentleness. The expression encourages me and I try again, alternating gestures—scowls and frowns, simpers and smiles, gasps of fear or bewilderment.

Soon enough, the answer is clear and I relax my countenance, prodding it lightly with my fingertips. I cannot do anything about this. The elves' magic only permits me to gesture as they prefer—to smile, to be joyful—and nothing else.

A dreadful silence settles around me, my thoughts stalled into hesitation. My fingers weave gently, resting upon the romantic tutu, gaze averted from the mirror.

The clock ticks high above and light flickers at the end of the shelf. That woman's voice returns—or, perhaps, I finally pay attention to it again—and I force myself to focus on descending from the music box to travel towards her.

Resolved but utterly scared, I breathe a few times and approach the box's edge. Kneeling gracefully, I grip the decorated rim before sliding my pointe flats to graze the first step.

Its surface is glazed, and I cling to an ornament for dear life. My heaving whooshes around me, but my gaze centres on the next step. That one is easier, the following is comfortable, and the last two are almost rhythmical.

I reach the floor emboldened, smoothing my romantic tutu albeit the gesture is fruitless; the ceramic remains as perfect and firm as my features. Apparently, only a few actions are allowed, all charming and desired by the elves—no wrinkles, no sadness, no lack of elegance.

Shaking those ideas away, I listen to the voice and move cautiously. My first steps are as delicate as my jeté, and I test the wood not to splinter my ceramic-made flats.

Slowly, the voice grows louder and more defined, oblivious to my approach. Crossing through some open ring cases, I watch my reflection faceted in a diamond and rounded in a ruby, all while pondering whether my incipient speech is enough to communicate with this refined lady. I pass a tiny locket inside a glass protector, and when she giggles again I halt abruptly, listening.

It takes me a moment to understand, but the truth is evident —it's not *one* voice, but *two*, so attuned and similar they are almost indistinguishable. They murmur and hush, intertwining as if their conversation were a perfect song.

Enticed by this minor discovery, I amble carefully until reaching a stack of leather-bound books. Veering left, I mince silently through the narrow edge of shelf between the spines and the glass door while looking ahead of me. Not far away there is a broad space between the volumes, and lights emanate bronze-coloured from between them. The gaps' secrets reflect blurry in the cupboard's doors—and I struggle not to gasp in surprise.

The books hide a single-room dollhouse, and two porcelain

figurines stand inside! Their shapes blur in their reflection on the glass doors, but their svelte bodies are unmistakable.

I take a few steps onward but halt, hands clasped gently near my chest. I was eager and wanted to rush towards them, yet now I hesitate. They surely don't want anyone interrupting their lively conversation. What could I offer them? They have this beautiful room for themselves, while I'm... just a curious nuisance.

My hesitation roots me in place for a long moment, but my treacherous legs carry me forward with dainty steps, point first with proper form. My unwilling pace slows near the last spine— a thick one made of soft velvet and gilded in silver—and my fingertips indulge in its softness while I muster my courage.

Prodding my unchanging dress and updo, I tap thrice on that velvety book to signal my presence. The voices halt immediately, gasping and gossiping between them.

"Yes?" One asks, curious.

"It's the new ballerina!" The other whispers audibly. She hums after a pause, clearing her throat and amiably calling, "Come, little lady. We want to meet you."

A smile trembles on my lips, as anxious as I am, but my good manners carry me across the edge to bow down. My gaze etches on the floor while they giggle, whispering in a foreign language, each sound punctuated with the irks of excitement and delight. Someone moves, fabric shushes, and porcelain shrieks. Ugly; cracking.

The noise upsets me and I raise to look around the dollhouse room.

It is a library lined with miniature books, jingles, jewels, and copper pottery; its back wall is decorated in gold, and the floor carpeted in a pale tan. Two figurines stand in the centre, tall and thin—porcelain-made twins, dressed in skillfully sculpted silk embellished with filigree. Their pale rose hair is long, tangled into the bookshelf and reaching the floor, and I follow the coils to—

A gasp. It escapes me, so shocked I cannot prevent it. My treacherous feet take one step back, my gaze etching impolitely on their hands—melded together, abraded and blended into an amorphous, fingerless mass.

I want to move, to escape, to chassé away into my music box… yet I keep watching, horrified at the twins before me.

Rightmost's nose is flattened, her cheeks scarred with sanding marks, streaking up to her forehead and stretching to the side I can't see. Leftmost's mouth is crooked and half-sanded, her visible eye chipped into blindness. Her nostrils were broken and the repair job was done in common clay and with the skill of a brutish toddler.

Tempos pass in awful silence. They watch me, oh so proper yet oh so knowing—as if the horror were visible beneath my ~~enforced~~ smile.

"P-pleasuh to meet-t you," I urge myself to mutter, unintelligibly yet forcing that neutral countenance I saw on my reflection. The magic aides me, puffing my face into an adorable, coy gesture.

Rightmost nods with courtly acceptance, shoulders jittering in delight. "You are kind, little ballerina. But we see…" She cocks the head, smiling gently while finding her words. "—we understand the… *curiosity* in your features, even under that perfect smile."

She trails off as I avert my gaze, fixated on the scattered trinkets and embarrassed to look at them. How did they uncover my shock if my face doesn't gesture freely?

"It is a simple story," Leftmost comments unsolicited and without reproach, turning slightly towards me. "We were gifted to the elven mother when she was a child, but she was clumsy and dropped us. Then, when crying at our broken chips, she used her tears to blend magic into clay and fix my nose."

"And paint your eye!" Rightmost titters with genuine amusement. "After that, the elf didn't dare to restore *me,* but kept us here. She never lets the boy touch us." Her last words ring somewhat bitter and a silence stretches. It is yearning, warmed by the figurine's fond smile. "But you know? Even decades after, she keeps visiting and saying we are perfect as we are."

A lie, I realise, remaining silent while thinking of an excuse to leave.

"That-t is lo-vely," I stutter after a while, mispronouncing both by my inability and my horror. I want to depart, to escape and return to my gorgeous space! "Ap-polo...gies. I must retuhn- to my moo-sic box," I smile apologetically, without considering whether the spells allow it.

The twins glance at each other and lean in unison.

"Come again," Leftmost says, gentle and almost motherly. "We will wait for you. There is much to talk about."

I bow deeper than upon my arrival, yet it takes all my restraint to retreat elegantly; my heart pounds frantically, and I purse my trembling lips to contain a gasp of fear. These twins have no place in this world of beauty, and their mere presence is simply jarring. Why would the mother keep them? It must be pity or an act of commiseration because, otherwise, these two would be destroyed.

Stalling my thoughts, I measure the first steps out of the nook, taking one every other heartbeat. Then, I turn through the book's spines, manage four carefully controlled moves, and leap through the shelf, running to my music box and balancing my feet not to stumble near it. With my heart pounding recklessly, I count eleven exhalations and crawl through the staircase towards the dance floor.

Why do the sisters bother me so much? Their faces were horrifying, but they seemed... almost amused at their brokenness; accepting of it, even. *Am* I terrified by them? Or by the prospect of whatever happened to them? Or perhaps... the fear of one day being broken and aged like so? Would the elven boy love me in that case?

Shaking my head to scatter those thoughts, I reach the dance floor's centre and wait.

Through the darkness of the night and my thoughts, isolated as the other voices ripple in the room. Through that loneliness, I wait.

My breathing is more stable by the morning, so I stand, prodding my updo and my romantic tutu. My elongations are short and useful, enough to warm my body and distract me from last night. Just like the other days, I wait in second position, but the day is idle and the afternoon quiet, the room closed and isolated from the world that brims outside that window.

A few following nights casts me into restless sleeps, chased by nightmares of chipped ceramic and the sisters' unwanted fix. Forgetting isn't easy, so I invest my nights to imagine what enchanting poses I will display for the boy on the next day—and thus I settle into a boring routine.

Three out of six days, he comes to the room and watches me dance for the briefest of moments. Those tempos are magical and exhilarating, but they fade quickly, leaving me empty. I yearn for more, wishing it deeply... but ignore what it is, unable to feel it, least of all explain it with my limited words.

Some days, the boy retrieves a book or a clockwork device and spends the entire morning enthralled by whatever object he picked until the mother calls him. The other three are quiet and relaxed, and I use them to dance to my own tune, singing and improving my speech... but dissatisfaction grows steadily, fed by this dull routine.

It's been a month since my arrival, and the sealed cabinet on the other wall catches my attention. It is dark and foreboding, and I dread whatever could be found inside if those mangled sisters were in this open, beautiful cupboard. The thought sours me but I shake my head, closing my eyes and focusing on my breathing —I have much to do, and cannot dally because of those thoughts.

The door will soon open. The boy will soon come.

To me, he will come.

Elated, I plié into first position, arms bending above my updo and settle to wait.

After a few tempos, the boy enters the room and darts towards the cupboard, gaze etched on the door's knobs. He twists once and it does not bulge, twice and the desperation to set me to dance takes over. The doors rattle the more he tries, each time with growing ~~frustration~~ fervour until the entire cupboard quakes under his eager, ungainly motions.

Fear creeps within me as the furniture protests, rattling in place just like my music box does—but I sustain my first position, a lovely smile firm in my features, my ~~dread~~ enthusiasm building.

The doors finally creak open, and the boy plunges towards my music box with an eagerness that ~~startles me~~ warms my heart. His amethyst coat covers my field of view, its gold embroidery diffusing the morning's light as he picks the box's winding key and turns it ~~(so rough, so rough and fast)~~.

It rolls once, and I inhale.

It shrieks redoubled, and I think of my movements.

It winds up and sticks in place, straining the mechanism as the boy fiddles with it. ~~Groaning~~. Nervous, anxious. Desperate to set me to dance. His movement is brutish, sharp, ungainly. He mumbles something I cannot understand, and his cheeks puff with effort to—

His hand jerks from the winding key, hitting the box's side and rattling my word. It tumbles violently... (or do I?), and I lose my balance (why?) to stumble across the dance floor. The lid ululates behind me, looming as if falling on top—and when I swirl, my ankle catches on the box's edge, and I plunge into the shelf's floor.

I'm ~~not~~ falling. I'm ~~not~~ falling.

"Help me, help me! ~~Protect me!~~" Those words repeat while I drop, unsupported, hovering in an unending fermata, time stretching like a caesura.

The emptiness is unbearable, swarming and paralysing. I'm helpless, plummeting, the boy's ~~silent~~ scream reverberating all-encompassing, watching me sink with ~~amused~~ terrorised emerald eyes.

The end nears, and a figment of my mind hollers for help—but my face remains stuck on that gentle smile, hands poised in an adage.

The noise is shallow. Muted and dry, echoing to wood. I lay on the shelf's floor, my body stilled, arms stretched in second position, feet en pointe and ready to dance.

It didn't happen to me.

I didn't fall.

I'm not in pain.

The tingles in my back are just anxiety; the stiffness on my shoulder blades is due to my poor stretches. It is my ~~his~~ fault.

"Help me, ~~save me~~," I wish to say, but the words won't come, and my smile stays on.

Tempos pass idle while the music slowly creeps towards me. It tingles, mellow, and I imagine myself performing a plié, a pirouette, following the notes as they unfold.

A shadow looms over me and I turn, smiling genuinely at the

boy. He is ~~smirking~~ terrified, hands quivering as they approach me.

"Help me! Please! ~~Leave me alone!~~" I beg in silence, feeling the gentleness of his walnut fingers curling around my waist. I smile because he came for me, moving me with care, heaving, scowling at my figure and grazing my hand with his large fingertip. The shelf obscures his face, but he returns me to the music box, hovering my body over the dance floor.

Slothfully, my toes reach the mirror's surface, and I settle into first position before raising my arms. The elven boy chuckles, gigantic hands cupped to shield me as I stand on my own.

The box's music is dwindling, but I advance and retreat, tuning a few pirouettes because my back isn't hurting ~~(liar!)~~ and my legs are ~~not~~ (un?)damaged. I test an arabesque, my supporting leg standing firm, the other raised behind in a flawless, straight line. I switch into a croisé and dance, reassured.

I am *not* broken, and the boy sighs with relief, clapping and giggling.

I'm ~~awful~~ beautiful, and I whirl and leap, legs perfectly split because there is no pain ~~(it hurts!)~~.

The music ends in a slow descent, and I reach the centre, casting a révérence and meeting the boy's gaze with an immaculate smile.

Did my ballet please him? Why is he frowning? Don't frown! Is he scowling at me? What did I do wrong? I'll dance some more!

A frown ripples on his forehead, lips pursing into a dot. My gaze halts on his eyebrows, tight like his pout. I shiver, fearful, aware of the truth.

I am ~~not~~ broken. I can dance; I just did it for him!

The boy snatches me with his left, his right hand fetching the music box. I cling to him, to everything I've known so far—but it doesn't matter. Nothing matters; not how my mind screams, and not the overpowering fear coursing through me.

I'm powerless. At his mercy.

Watching the detailed floor rush by, his coat flapping with each step. My arms brace his fingers while I gasp, terrified of falling again.

A thud, firm against the wood. Contorting my neck, I see my music box on the doorless bookcase, placed in a gap on a higher level. He stretches the hand holding me, leading me into that shelf but the window's light blinds me, burning my eyes and my thoughts. The height dizzies me, but soon my feet graze the familiar glass of the dance floor, and I stumble to regain balance while the boy's footfalls rush towards the door.

It creaks open and closed, fulminating like the window's light.

I stay here, on this secondhand bookcase. Alone and shivering.

Conscious that my smile is lovely and empty. Aware that I am valueless. Broken. *Worthless.*

I haven't moved since the boy misplaced me on this incorrect bookcase. I've waited for him in first position and ready to dance... but he hasn't returned, each passing moment hastening my heartbeat and feeding my distress.

The wind ululates into the room, distracting me, and I see the silky curtains flowing into the inside—scented, sweet and earthy, the sheer fabric toying with the light.

The view sours me. This secondhand bookshelf is *not* my place; I belong to the pretty cupboard of fine figurines, not here.

Sighing in distress, I shift my weight from one foot to another, annoyed that *my* clumsiness and poor balance resulted in that ~~shallow fall~~ stumble. I'm a ballerina and should have performed better.

Scared of whatever would happen now, I watch my shivering hands, stretching them to the sides... but apprehension seizes me nonetheless.

Are any splinters in my body? Something I didn't see? Am I chipped? ~~Valueless?~~

My trembling turns into a violent shake, and I stretch my hands all too carefully. Terrified of slamming and breaking them, I assess the fingers and their glazing, finding no chips. Arching my back, I twist and gaze at my svelte figure. My legs seem perfect, the pointe flats are pristine, and both dress and updo are as intricate and delicate as always.

I feel... *something* but it's *not* pain, just... too much ballet. The exhaustion and weariness of the moment. I have been training ceaselessly, holding postures for too long without stretching or relaxing—and that awareness convinces me of elongating.

The motions are simple and gentle at first, one arm, the other, a leg in arrière, then derrière. Dreading to hear shrieking ceramic, I lunge left and right, slowly easing into splits. Then, I bend back and forth until ~~the pain subsides~~ I'm reacquainted with my body and ready for more.

Standing, I tiptoe towards a corner with slippery anxiety yet covering each angle—trying pliés, tendus, and pirouettes. I whirl, humming a melody and twirling again. My concerns vanish as I fouetté until the music flows through me, and my grand adage is a testament to my balance and control.

Only after much capitulation do I settle into a second position. I don't want the boy to find me lazing in the velvet sleep compartment; I am a ballerina, regardless of this unfortunate misplacement, and will remind him of my grace and value.

He'll return to this room, rush to this bookcase, and undoubtedly take me to my rightful cupboard.

Being misplaced here is just a small, deserved penalty; I should've done better.

The dusk dwindles, streams of amethyst light seeping through the curtains into the listless silence of the room. The clock's rhythmic sound draws my attention; its ticking accounts for the hours that passed without the boy returning. It distresses me, counting the time that has no right to pass so incomplete and musicless.

A few more ticks, and the night slips into the room. The moment everything is in shadows is the moment the cabinets awake with sparkling lights and distant voices, their merriment so foreign to me.

I am here. On this incorrect bookshelf, alone on my dance floor.

Worry consumes me while I soften my stance into a soft relevé (it is my fault, I know it!), but a realisation dawns moments after. This is just a *temporal* change, not a permanent one. It's only a matter of catching the boy's attention to show him that I have learned from my mistake, and that I can still dance.

A genuine grin curls on my lips, my hands clasping delicately as I look around the box. Roguish, my gaze settles on the winding key, teasing me with an idea.

I could find a way to twirl it a few times, start the music, and dance on my own. The boy is bound to come to me after that!

The idea takes root, but my right foot steps back, aware of the risk it entails. I could damage myself, reducing my value in the process... yet I'm willing to do so.

Decided, I relax my limbs, shake my arms and prod my immutable hairdo. Then, I mince through the mirrored dance floor into the corner where the lever is. Kneeling and holding to the gilded edge, I stretch a leg back as a counterweight and peer at the gigantic handle—gold-made, thin and rounded, spiralling twice before ending on the flattened circle the elves grip.

I could leap onto the winding key, hang from it and let my whole weight move it, but doing so would scratch my glazing. In turn, standing on the flattened circle would require an inordinate balance not to fall and shatter... which I already demonstrated not to have.

The lack of a solution is frustrating, and so I sit on my ankles, glancing around this bookcase in defeat. In one tempo I'm staring around, but in another emptiness engulfs me—tightening my throat, upsetting my breathing, and muting my limited voice.

A thought swirls to the forefront, irrefutable. I am alone. I have nobody to ask for help, no friends or acquaintances. There is no light in this book-filled level, no noises, or movement except the rusty old scent of inked pages no longer read. This loneliness rings truthful, just like the other thoughts cavorting within me.

I can't do this; not on my own and not without help.

"I am a c-coward," I gasp, repeating the words each time more frantic than before. "Coward, and a-alone."

Coward. Alone. Coward. Alone. *Coward*. **Alone**.

"Help—p... me," I mumble, desperate, tears boiling within me. "I c-can't d-do this!"

My hands land on my knees while I sob, heaving and hiccuping; my mouth opens round, eyes slimming into half-moons—but the reflection on the dance floor remains immaculate, smooth and utopian, polished and gracious. It frightens me even more until my heart pounds like drums chasing a crescendo, the fear oh so certain, oh so truthful—yet, once again, the mirror-reflected features remain perfectly relaxed, mellow and orderly.

I despair, feeling a grimace within me even when my smile arches lovingly. I quiver in fear, but it looks demure, and when I gasp, my cheeks blush tenderly.

My feelings are so at odds with my reflection, so out-of-tune that I doubt them. Perhaps the misery swarming me isn't real? ~~But it drowns me!~~ Maybe it is just an illusion? ~~But it throttles me!~~

"Mademoiselle?" A rough baritone slithers through the shelves, questioning. Almost concerned. "Ma brave dame, where are you?"

I whimper quietly, wincing in shame. That voice is not

talking to me; who would want to address me? Embarrassed, I cross a hand over my mouth to swallow all sobbing.

"Don't be shy, mademoiselle," the baritone repeats, resonating from my right. It's on this same level, perhaps hidden between the books. "I saw you being moved here today! Thanks to my glasses!" He chuckles, and metal creaks. "I'm—agh!" Paper slides and tumbles, echoing around and muting angry words. "My apologies, these books are—agh! Oh!"

Sitting on my ankles, I keen my hearing to find any more clues about this voice. He appears to be in a distressing situation, but there is a lightness in his tone I cannot quite place. Slowly, like a développé, that sadness skulking in my mind fades away, transformed into curiosity by these anonymous troubles.

Abruptly, something wooden rolls and tumbles, and a few words brim staccato with the clear cadence of swearing. I chuckle at the intonation, so irrevocable and certain.

"Mademoiselle! Would you—?" He chokes and paper feathers as if scattered on the breeze. "—être dans la merde! Ouch! Will the—?" Another muted, leathery sound ripples through, slashing the man's words.

Wincing at the remnant echoes, I stand and wait, suspicious of what is happening. He seems in dire distress, assailed by a terrible situation… but something in his intonation reminds me of a façade. A performance; staged to lure me in… but to what purpose?

Undecided—and too keen to forego my sadness for a moment—I cross my hands behind my back, frowning in my imagination. Soon enough, a few more books tumble and fall, and I flinch when glass shatters.

"Ma brave dame! Would you—?" More paper slides and the male figure grunts, evidently in despair. "Help! A—agh!" His voice thins into a gulp.

I gasp, concerned, mouth quivering and barely shaping the

sounds. "Mon-nsieur?" I hesitate, concerned about my pronunciation and hoping he won't agree. "Help—p? Me?"

Would I even be capable of providing any assistance? What if he damages me?

"Oui, s'il vous plaît!" He shouts just before wood tumbles and falls, evidently confusing my intentions.

Noises clatter around the place, but the other cabinets don't seem perturbed. The entire situation is odd, and my personal struggles seem so irrelevant compared to the baritone's distress that I find myself—thoughtlessly so—descending the music box's steps.

I elongate on the rack's wooden floor and smooth my immutable romantic tutu as if to gain some time—but when something else seems to tumble off a rack, I finally mince towards the voice. My back aches, but I refrain from rubbing it not to scratch the ceramic; it is just my anxiety, and nothing more.

Paper continues to shush and whoosh as I move, but the noises have a distinct cadence; a pattern, not melodious but definitely purposeful. A blend of emotions blossom with this realisation, contradictory and unintelligible as feeling both dread and eagerness can be. I keep moving, dainty yet oscillating between trepidation and nosy puzzlement.

I stop now and then to glimpse at the books' spines or even doubt my actions—yet whenever I do so something tumbles in the nook between the books, and I hurry again, skipping gently ahead. The light coming from it flickers and fades, sometimes brighter, sometimes dimmer, yet certainly quieter than before.

The last book before the edge is a thick, encased volume of black leather with silver details. I hold onto it for longer than needed, slowly leaning forwards while wishing not to find someone as broken as the sisters—but the nook inside is entirely different to theirs.

This is a doll-sized, narrow library with miniature books

perfectly aligned on each side. The back is shaped like a window illuminated with magic, the glass polished and clean. There is a desk against that wall, the surface pristine and devoid of clutter, the baritone's owner standing atop it.

He's carved from ebony, dressed in a formal suit, and perched on a gold-made cane. His hair is neatly trimmed, and he wears squarish, dark-framed glasses that graze his populated moustache. He's looking regally at the shelf ahead, completely oblivious that his tie is stuck to the shelf behind him, stretched across the space as if pushed by a non-existent wind.

"Mademoiselle!" He cheers, trying to bow.

His tie pulls him back tightly and he gasps, dropping the cane and clutching his neck. Swearing between gritted teeth, he pulls the tie free, fabric shrieking as he bows to me.

"Welcome, welcome!" He repeats, hopping to the chair and onto the floor. "I'm pleased to meet you!"

I révérence, unsure of how to act. "Bons-uh." Embarrassed by my pronunciation, I clear my throat and try again, "Bonsoir." It tumbles a little less misshapen, almost making me proud of myself.

"Good evening, indeed!" He chirps, approaching and bowing again. "You have such a lovely voice! You should use it more!" He smiles, sliding a hand through his buzzed black hair.

"Thank-k you," I whisper, still doubtful but enunciating correctly. The situation is awkward, and my stuttering may also be a reflection of my embarrassment. "I'm... L-Lyra," I offer, touching my chest before gesturing towards him. "Your-s? M-monsieur?"

"André. Others call me Warlock, but don't let them scare you!" He chuckles, beaming with amusement before clearing his throat. "I believe you need my help, ma brave dame?" His eyes of obsidian twinkle with delight.

His comment takes me aback, and I tilt my head to one side, looking at the shelves again. The wood is polished to a mirror, every book is in position, and the desk only has a few neatly organised trinkets. The nook is pristine and devoid of the consequences of the prior mayhem.

"*You...* asked-d for *my* help-p," I stutter, not even attempting to frown in confusion. "This... is not-t brok-ken."

Did he deceive me? To which purpose?

His face is far more expressive than mine, and he wiggles the brows and moustache before curtseying with an exaggerated flourish. "I lied," André confesses, roguish and unashamed. "You wouldn't have come otherwise," he lingers, spectacles sliding down. "—and likely scurried away from me if I approached uninvited."

Heat crawls through me, and when I touch my cheeks, the cold ceramic tells me I'm grinning. Evidently, embarrassment is also not worth displaying.

Bobbling his head, André giggles and rolls a hand, encouraging an answer I rather not give.

"I don't... want-to imp-pose..." I take a few steps back. I don't like being deluded and will not receive his pity. I am not ~~broken~~ helpless, and can try something else on my own. "B-but I... appreciate your... p-proposal."

André waits for a few tense tempos. "Fair enough, mademoiselle," he says after a while, extending a hand towards the nook's entrance. "But I'll walk you back to your music box."

Since there is no other choice, and certain he will attempt something later, I dip my head and fall into step beside him. After only a few tempos of silent walking, André begins a monologue I can barely follow. My thoughts are skirmishing, trying to discover how to dispatch him upon arrival, but... I keep giggling at his jests. Soon enough, I'm caught up on the tales of the many books he's read—most about gemstones and magic.

The journey is amusing, and André doesn't seem capable of

remaining silent. We stroll calmly, and the talk is so engaging that the path stretches until my suspicions are gone. He pushes the spectacles up at intervals, scatters to talk about books, gestures exuberantly, and makes me laugh—all while I ponder how to ask for his help after I so unkindly denied it.

"I couldn't read! It was... effrayant!" André says as we walk. He shakes his head, and the spectacles slide down his nose again. "But then I got these, and the letters returned to me!"

"How did... get-them?" I stutter, beckoning to his frames.

André's chuckle vanishes my embarrassment, and he pushes his spectacles up. A spiral forms on the glass, enlarging his obsidian eyes.

"The elven woman is an *excellent* sorcerer!" He indicates the distant door, smiling fondly; his ebony creaks and wrinkles like an old man's face. "It is ungainly, but I was panicking, mademoiselle. The words had departed me most suddenly, and I was unable to read and... too ashamed to disclose my ailment." A coy, prudent smile curls his lips, but he rolls a hand, dismissing himself. "But the elf noticed and gave me these!"

"The m-mothuh?" I ask, prying and impolite.

"Oui en effet!" André chuckles, wiggling the moustache before smoothing his jacket. "I believe she enchanted some earrings to craft them. These crystals changed my way of seeing this world."

I tilt my head, considering his words, when I realise something else—this conversation feels as pre-arranged as his feigned call for help. Is there something he wants to tell me? Something... I'd never have asked otherwise? I want to pout in distress, anxious at being coached in this manner—but my lips move into a curious grin.

Resigned, yet intrigued nonetheless, I whisper, "What-t chang-ged?"

"My perception, mademoiselle!" André scrunches his wide nose to move the spectacles up. "For years I took for granted my ability to read, enjoying book after book without taking a moment to be grateful for it…" His baritone softens as my bewilderment becomes obvious. "You see, mademoiselle, life and time tend to take some things away. Even from us, figurines. Unfortunately, it is only when we lose them that we realise their true value."

Our pace slows almost on cue, and my follow up question scatters to oblivion as André gasps in awe at my music box. It is a large circle of gold filigree, the domed lid pulled up to create the mirrored wall I use to watch my positions. He hums approvingly, twirling one side of his moustache before darting towards the lever.

I try to stop him, gesturing an arrière adage, but his name stumbles never-spoken in my mind. André runs, gasping in delight, glowing with child-like curiosity and muttering in different languages. He circles the box twice in each direction before crouching near the winding key.

It takes him a long moment, but he glances at me, his frames sliding again. I hesitate, tinkering with my fingertips near my navel and glimpsing at the key—yet he chuckles, delighted, winking with one eye and turning back to the box, a hand twisting his moustache with pensive determination.

"This is easy!" He exclaims after several tempos, scratching his chin. "I cast a coiling spell, place it on the winding key, and we dance around it in as many turns as you want to wind it up." André sounds didactic, gesturing with two fingers as if those were us. "Then, we seal it with a word, and when the morning comes…"

"I s-speak, and m—music flows?" My question is embarrassingly stammered and ashamed. I denied him before, yet somehow he remains willing to help me.

André nods eagerly. "I have enough magic for that!" He confirms, bowing elegantly and clapping his hands as if to encourage me to proceed.

Instead of answering, I look down in shame. I... should have been kinder to him. He seemed to want nothing else than to assist me.

"T-thank y-you," I manage, the whisper as small as myself.

André smiles, genuine and kinder than before. "It's my pleasure, mademoiselle." His baritone lingers as he stretches a hand, palm up and inviting. "Now, shall we? We will find the magic word as we waltz."

I gawk at him, perplexed by his eagerness to solve my conundrum; I never apologised and now stare at him, confused by his kindness, and distraught by my own actions... yet unsure of what to do. Understanding glimmers in André's dark eyes, and he wiggles his bushy brows until I titter. It eases me enough to tiptoe closer, taking on the joy radiating from him; it pushes away that part of me that reminds me of the fall and how I disembarked in this bookcase.

Yet without any further delays we dance the night away, laughing so loudly my heart forgets its misery. We whirl around the lever, my ceramic chiming in trebles, his ebony wood stomping dryly. He chants the word and I repeat it, giggling and lifting a weight off my shoulders with every time I mention it.

It seems interminable, the waltz and the joy... but eventually the dawn coats the room's far wall and André departs, curtseying and skipping to his nook with a curious gait.

Already warm from so much dancing, I prod my updo and tutu and climb to stand in the middle of my dance floor. I balancé sideways for a while, shifting my weight gracefully from one foot to the other to shake away the nervousness André's departure has left me with. My heart pounds like a drum booming allegro, but my confidence stabilises as I lower into a grand plié before settling in second position.

The clock ticks in the ensuing silence, but my wait is shorter than expected—after a few moments, the mother's earthy scent appears near the door.

Ready to dance, I whisper the magic word, "Audace!"

The box's mechanisms creak and shirr, and the music sparks alive.

Closing my eyes, I tiptoe around my dance floor, ignoring the rest of the world—nothing else matters except my ballet. I'm twirling, flowing with the melody when the door shrieks open in the distance. Someone gasps and I adage, elven footfalls fading away while I sway here and there, smiling as the steps return doubled.

I'm counting my fouettés when the boy's emerald eyes glow near my shelf. He admires me, gasping and clasping when I leap in and perform a flawless split. His astonishment revitalises me, erasing my worries and reassuring me that all will be well.

The enchantment wanes and the music decreases ralentando, so I pirouette once more, ending in a final révérence. My heart pounds harshly, and my legs almost falter from the expectation —but he turns, the mother's silhouette occupying most of my field of view.

I fret, still poised and regal, holding my pose because this is my only chance. Was my ballet satisfactory? Will they leave me? Please, I danced for you! I'll do better! I'll keep improving! That stumble was nothing!

They speak, but the sounds don't reach me.

They move, and I panic—but soon, the boy claps, leaning towards me.

I barely notice his smile before his walnut hand stretches and opens, fingers as thick as my body. His grip is ~~rough~~ gentle as he lifts me away from my music box, and I hang to his fingers, legs intertwined, smiling charmingly albeit panic overwhelms me.

Then he walks. With me, and across the room. Meanwhile, two thoughts scream in my mind.

~~Don't throw me!~~ I can still dance for you, boy!

The boy walks with gigantic steps, turquoise coat fluttering behind him, gold embroidery sparkling with the morning's light. His grip is ~~too tight~~ firm, and it ~~hurts~~ holds me securely. I clutch his topmost fingers, batting my ceramic eyelashes in sheer terror, my petal peplum flowing beneath his hand.

Wasn't I good enough? I tried! I will try harder!

~~Don't drop me, don't drop me!~~

I close my eyes, feeling the boy's footfalls drum the floor—but my heart beats louder and faster. My arms brace his fingers, seeking purchase.

"Forgive me!" I scream, shaping my mouth—yet my perfect, courtly features display nothing, my voice non-existent.

Desperate, I tilt my chin, offering the best smile. My hands are poised, and my toes move en pointe to show him ~~I'm not broken~~ that the ballet is intrinsic to me—so much that I wound that key on my own! ~~Liar!~~ To start the box just to dance for him! He must understand my effort!

A door shrieks ajar close by, and I open my eyes at the familiar noise. *My* cupboard meets me, gigantic and cosy, and joy overwhelms me; it transforms my smile into an honest gesture, and warmth fills my heart as my box lands on its righteous place—that same level the boy assigned me upon arrival. The mother's purple nails reflect the box's gold filigree as she holds it still while he stretches his arm to hover me over the mirrored floor.

Bending my knees, I make room before tiptoeing, delicately finding the dance area to settle in a soft relevé. The boy's youthful fingers shield me protectively while the mother twirls the winding key with incredible gentleness. The music unfolds with every turn, tickling like languid raindrops in a stately andante; I unfurl in an adage still shielded within the boy's protective fingers. When the melody settles in a classy moderato, the surrounding hands retreat and the boy watches me with expectant emerald doe-eyes.

I tease him with a développé, unfolding my leg to extend it alongside the music, to flourish away from the panic rattling my insides. Fear isn't something the elves want to see, and thus my face cannot (must not) show it.

The motion soothes me, the ballet embracing me with its many truths. I will dance for him ~~because that's what I'm meant to do;~~ as many times as he wants because that is my only goal and purpose—to ensure his happiness, to distract him from his woes. I will dance for the elves again and again, now and forever, whenever they want and how they want. Whichever tune plays on the box, I'll show the boy I can master it and won't give him a reason to throw me away.

I move into an arabesque, rising and tiptoeing in tandem with the music, so delicate and nimble the boy claps and skips in amusement. I lose myself in the melody, stretching the moment, pirouetting and leaping, swaying alongside the tune until I finally révérence, the quivers that rattle my heart held tightly behind a romantic smile.

The boy bows to me when the last harmonics are still echoing around... yet there is something in his gaze. He straightens to close the cupboard's glass door before I can understand his ~~contempt~~ gesture, and the shelf above me hides his face.

Desperate but poised, I seek for other signs of approval—a smile, a nod, anything else. Nothing suffices until I hear his calm breathing, his movements tranquil and normal. Does that mean he's pleased? Did I awe him? Am I enough?

Worry eats me from the inside, yet my cheeks blush and puff, my lips pressed into a demure, flirty smile. A few tempos pass by, the elves exchange a few silent words before departing without even speaking to me. Their secrecy numbs my mind, and I stay in that final révérence after the door shrieks closed—waiting for them to return, to grant me their approval, to praise my dance.

One moment I blink and the noon's shimmer now illuminates the glass piece over the table but my breathing is still rattled, my panting excessive as I wonder what that soreness on my legs is—then flutter my eyelashes to discard the thought.

The truth is simple. I danced too much with André and clearly I held that révérence for hours; I haven't rested enough. ~~I'm not broken; this isn't pain~~.

A yawn overtakes me but it is gentle, my legs carrying me into a few coy spins—to unwind like the music box, to dismiss the quivering tickling in my ceramic. Arching my back for a stretch, I exhale my anxiety while wondering whether to rest now that I'm home; rest and practice my balance to impress the boy when he returns in a few days.

The idea entices me, and I lazily tiptoe towards the bed compartment. Each step brings a world of emotions, and as I move, my thoughts wander into the many choreographies I could develop to please the boy—until my reflection stops me.

~~Marred. Chipped.~~

"No!" I fret, immobilised by a dark speck on my waist. "No, no, no!"

I can't be broken; it is simply impossible! That nuisance on my back is imperceptible, not real, not felt. It's due to dancing nonstop and the distressing situation I just went through. I am *not* damaged or the boy wouldn't have returned me to *the* cupboard!

Desperate, I near the open mirrored lid and sit on my ankles, back towards the mirror. My ballerina's flexibility allows me to twist—peplum spread like a blossoming flower, profile graceful and courtly, cheeks slightly blushed. My gaze seeks the reflection until that speck comes into sight—rough and unpainted, carved in my waist, sized like those tears I want to cry but can't release.

A spasm ripples through my back and that speck creaks, a few crevices extending from its corners. Creaking. Shrieking. Demoting me.

~~I'm broken, valueless.~~

My breathing rags, my vision narrows—but realisation settles.

The mirror is dirty from the relocation. ~~I'm defective, worthless.~~ Yes, yes, that must be it! I'm perfect and whole, unmarred and agile. ~~But my back ached while dancing.~~ I pirouetted perfectly, astonishing the boy with my nimbleness and grace.

This is *not* a chip, just dirt from that awful bookcase I was put on.

Thoughtless and emotionless, I fall to my hands, heaving with dizziness, watching the afternoon pass in silence— mournful and oblivious to my suffering.

The night arrives all too soon, and I spend it sitting on my heels in the middle of the dance floor. The following day fades in a blank second position, and its afternoon is as empty as the night —devoid of options.

I look at the room's door and wish the boy to return, but he does not visit me.

~~I'm too broken for him. Ugly and valueless.~~

It is not the right day. That must be it. I clearly lost count after being misplaced.

Two days later, the door creaks open and I beam, distress erased by the boy's beautiful smile. He comes to my cupboard, opens it gently, and sets me to dance before watching from afar, long braids falling past his shoulders.

I twirl and pirouette, daring the music and my body—beautiful and elegant, flowing alongside that melody, blossoming as it grows in a crescendo, and teasing him with shy balancés. I am proud of myself, of my grace and nimbleness, of my poise and manner... but after I révérence, the boy closes the cupboard doors without smiling.

His coldness is shocking, taking something vital away from me. It plunges me into a restless wait, and the morning flickers by while I stand in an arabesque, static and lonely. Every moment is unforgiving, the quietude bringing my attention to the sharpness ~~and that shameful chip~~ in my lower back.

My worries do not ease when I change into a third position, and neither when I tell myself it is just a minor nuisance; an itch, scarcely worth concern.

By noon, I am anxious. *Terrified.*

By the afternoon, I understand a truth embedded within me the moment that magic gave me life and set me to dance atop my music box.

There is nothing else in my existence except ballet.

Without it, I have no identity, no purpose, no reason to be here or anywhere. What do I do if I lose it? Who would I be? I am a ballerina, and that's all I am.

Panic floods me, and my arms tremble nonsensically as I melt into an inelegant stand. I wish those shivers would go away, that my balance would improve and my ballet would please the boy again.

For a few restless tempos, my gaze hops unruly from the box's ornaments to the glass doors, to the bookshelf, and back to my hands—now grazing the edge of my petal-like peplum.

The unbearable need for company surges within me and the idea of calling André warms my heart, but I close my eyes to perish the thought. His roombox is not on this cupboard, and the bookshelf is too far not to cause an ungainly racket while hailing him. I imagine myself pouting, chagrined, and retreat from the mirror not to see that gentle simper curling my lips—feeling it is enough.

By night, those abysmal thoughts return redoubled, and my legs quiver in a balancé just to usher them away. They do not leave me, instead lurking near, through the darkness.

The dusk flickers away and I descend the box's makeshift staircases while holding onto its gilded edges, one tiptoe at a time. The shelf's wooden floor remains as I remembered, and I test a few tendus pressured by the need to move.

My restlessness is unsettling, unnerving me. It encourages me to elongate, to swivel through the basics and improve enough to please the boy again—yet a voice stops as I'm beginning my mobility drills.

Distant, tenor and modulated, holding a perfect vibrato that ripples through the wood like a question—almost as if he were expecting someone would answer. The language is unknown to me, but it feels syllabic, soft and perfectly intertwined with harmonies I never heard before.

Hesitating, I tiptoe back and forth, utterly undecided until my curiosity takes over. I want to meet him, to learn whether his song is a duet... yet I worry unnecessarily. About this tenor singer, about the boy and my ballet, about my lack of balance and that detour to another bookshelf.

The questions stall me for several tempos, but when that fermata fades away I glide across the shelf in a silent demi-pointe —so absorbed that my back doesn't itch (it isn't real; it's not pain). Almost as if he'd heard me move, the man's tenor grows louder, singing in that musical mode so foreign to me.

There are no books on this side, just velvet cases and wooden boxes, some closed and others open to showcase jewellery that shimmers with magic. Carefully, I trace a path through the safest, broadest avenue, slowing and hastening in tandem with the tenor's song—until a large, rough stone blocks my advance.

I pause for a long moment, studying the rugged shapes and the edge near the shelf's end—sharp and blunt, clearly sliced and reflecting with the colours of the gemstone. A faint, yellowish light emanates from the inside, illuminating the path I should follow to cross that threshold and meet whoever lives there.

A shiver runs down my body, and I move closer with delicate piqués. I want to—

"Hello? Who is there?" His tenor is fascinating, silvery and flowing. The silence stretches while I don't reply, traipsing, but he hears me. "Are you the ballerina? Come! Be welcome!"

I jolt, gasping in surprise, fingers covering my mouth while shame fills me inside. How did he hear me? Was I so brutish? So inelegant? The embarrassment builds for a long moment, but as the silence develops that need for company I once felt returns redoubled—and I remember André's conversation, the warmth that embraced me as we danced, and the loneliness of the previous nights.

"Ap-pologies," I stammer, easing my breathing. "I did-n't want-to... intrude." The words slither with my sigh, my feet still in demi-pointe.

He chuckles, amused but polite. "Don't be shy, little ballerina. You aren't imposing! Come in!" A pause ensues, hesitant yet quiet, his voice less shiny when he adds, "I can't really go to you."

I want to frown but instead smile bashfully, my feet resuming those delicate piqués before I contemplate whatever shall I do. The rock's edge nears as the silence unfurls with anticipation; something wooden moves inside, silk shushing while a scent slithers soft and solemn. It entices me and I hurry, reaching the threshold, holding onto it and peering into the roombox.

The rock is a geode of smokey quartz, each crystal-like shelf filled with books, bamboo notes, and rolls. The tenor singer sits in the middle, dressed in a rich dress of heavy silk embroidered in gold and wearing a carmine coat. His hair is shaven to a fade on the sides but propped up at the top, and his angled eyes are narrow, sparkling welcomingly alongside his thin smile.

It takes me a few moments to realise that his hands are broken. One is raised, fingerless but balancing an incense cone on the palm, and the other only has the forefinger and half the thumb. He tilts slightly to face me, and I hear the strings inside his body tensing and squeaking—this man is a ball-jointed doll.

"Hello, little one!" This close, his tenor is even more fascinating, rich and vibrant like his curated smile. "It is lovely to meet you…" He dips his head in a courteous greeting. "—but you must excuse me, since I can't move from my chair to properly invite you inside."

"Ah y-you… hurt?" The words tumble out of my mouth and, as embarrassment paralyses me, the need to retreat in shame clogs my mind. Yet shame mustn't be shown; it could upset the elves. "I'm… I—"

His smile soothes me and I unwind, embarrassed—at my rudeness, at the trepidation of finding whether he is as broken as the sisters.

"Are you still learning to speak?" The jointed doll lingers, waiting for my meagre hum. "That explains much," he adds, tapping his leg with his only forefinger. "Stay, please. Perhaps you can practice speaking with me." Another pause, hesitant. "I will answer your questions if you do!"

Something within me hesitates, bewilderment startling my feet into one retreating step—but the heartache vibrating in his voice compels me to stay. He's lonely, just like me. The realisation hurts my heart and I nod, clasping my hands at the back.

"Am... l-learning," I whisper, anxious.

Smiling, he cranes his neck, letting me hear the old strings holding his body together. The sound startles me into blinking a few times and my gaze—rude, oh so rude—decants through his figure, following the gentle movement of his arms to land on the stillness of his legs. Understanding washes over him as I startle again, but he relaxes his shoulders, tilting his head as if my feelings—hidden under a polite resting smile—were clear to him.

"The strings moving my legs wore out long ago. I can't walk anymore; I'm too small to be re-tensed!" His tenor does not waver, and for half a tempo his angular, handsome countenance seems far older than what his sculpture shows. He doesn't seem upset, instead giggling gently. "The only thing I regret is that few figurines come here. The twins are locked in their box, but at least I get to sing with Margot!"

He laughs, and my face remains impassive, my scowl only imaginary. Days ago, I was lamenting nonsensically the ~~chip~~ dirty speck on my back, and this man here cannot walk nor use his hands. The memory of the sisters' mangled features swipes me and I shiver, a blend of emotions trapping me in silence. ~~Why are they here?~~ They are worse off than me. I shouldn't complain.

"What... hap-pened?" I stammer, fearful of asking because the truth could be harrowing.

"Life!" He laughs, stretching to place the incense atop a book, the silk of his long sleeves sliding and shushing. "You cannot survive life intact. That belief is the worst deception anyone can suffer." The man's voice softens, and he grins as if seeing right through me. "Life will chip you, little one. Crack or blind you. Fracture you, and leave its mark. It affects us all, except some do not want to accept it."

I hesitate, unsure of what he truly means. "That s-sounds... sage," I utter, embarrassed at the unfiltered thoughts.

He hums in agreement, pensive, strings stirring lazily. "Behati always says that one ages into wiseness, so you may be right... or you may not, as Gérard-dono argues." Smoothing his opulent dress, the jointed-doll gazes fondly to a small double portrait on a shelf—two figures standing around a woman with a long dress. "It may surprise you, little ballerina, but I'm old enough to have met the elven woman's mother. I—" A surprised gasp interrupts his words, bewilderment overtaking his features. "How rude of me! I haven't introduced myself! I'm Sougo, written like 'playing' and 'self'.* What is your name, little one?" He asks while bowing as deep as he can.

"The boy named me Lyra," I offer, hesitant—that day now belongs to a different era, and the innocent act of saying my name floods me with questions. "May..." I stutter, gaze glimpsing around the geode, my imbued properness berating me as I hesitate enough to whisper, "May I... ask you s-something?" A single question, I promise myself.

Sougo hums encouragingly, and that melodious sound calms my uneasiness.

"Why... did you say l-life... affects us?" I waver, my thoughts still dancing around his words. He said that life would fracture me and leave its mark, but that would drive the boy away from me. That thought... *horrifies* me.

---

* Author's Note: His name should be 遊吾 (Sō go), which is not (to my understanding) a traditional meaning... but neither it is to find dolls animated by magic. To me, self-reflection doesn't need to be always sombre, and thus this names reflects the idea of being creative with one's journey through life, especially as it takes some unseen twists and turns.

He smiles, wise and serene, his angled eyes curving into a fond smile. He looks at me as if I were a lost child, naïve and doe-eyed—yet sighs, his fingerless palm patting his hair.

"Because life isn't gentle, Lyra." Sougo's tenor is like a feather caressing my ceramic. "Life is an amalgam of people's stories, each struggling to accomplish something, to thrive or simply survive." He watches me with care, never pitying but as if aware of what my future may hold. "Those desires will affect you, even if they don't intend it. You cannot control *them*, only yourself... but doing so is akin to achieving a grand jeté; rewarding once achieved, yet terribly difficult to do so."

The sounds of silence dance between us for a long moment, the incense cone cackling and releasing its modest scent. I do not move, and Sougo doesn't hurry me for neither of us seems keen on breaking the delicate balance his words have delivered us into. My hands clasp on I think, my glazing smooth, my thoughts chipped ~~like my lower back~~ with distress—all swirling like ballet poses, each perfect on their own, their sequence a nonsensical mess.

"Is t-that why—?" I shuffle in place, uncomfortable because his words made me so. "Do you miss... walking?"

The question blurts out of me, uncontrollable as I flinch, averting my gaze in embarrassment. What was I thinking? Seeking further proof that I have no right to complain? I do not move nor apologise, stunned by my rudeness, while the new silence stretches like a caesura.

My heart beats desperately until Sougo sighs.

"Long ago, I panicked when my legs loosened and I began stumbling for the first time since elven magic gave me life," he confesses, the whisper honest and grave, never chastising. "I remember the desperation, the fear. The screams I couldn't shout, the terror I couldn't gesticulate..." Our eyes meet, that terror known to both of us—truthful but wordless, felt but never shown. "Losing my ability to walk was the irrefutable, unstoppable consequence. But do you know what ensued?" He waits for my negative hum, nodding before adding, "I survived and adapted into a more resourceful self. And when this happened —" Sougo gestures at his mangled hands "—I was prepared. Life isn't gentle, Lyra. Life... is just life."

I ~~grimace in desperation~~ smile oh so gently, not understanding.

"How c-can you... be so calm?" I whisper, stunned by his attitude, bewildered by that calmness that seeps through him. It isn't apathy; his features are too gentle and expressive, not vacant and gloomy. "Teach me. *Please.*"

My hands clasp on my chest, my plead silent and muted.

"I can't, Lyra." Sougo's tenor is apologetic, carrying the pain of a lifetime. "That calmness grows after ageing because time gives you a different perspective over past events... but it also comes from resilience. From understanding instead of shunning a part of you away." His voice softens, his smile knowing and mindful of my bewilderment. "Your feelings may spook you, but the serenity you seek will only come if you weather the storm of your emotions with the sole purpose of understanding them." He trails off, gesturing peacefully as if to reign himself. "It is like rehearsing for that grand jeté we mentioned before. You'll fail countless times until one day your leap is perfect and you are left with the task of mastering another, more challenging, one."

I don't answer him immediately; the words avoid me for a long moment.

Sougo waits for me, eventually turning to his incense and lighting a new one. "Would you come again, Lyra?"

"Perhaps," I curtsey, embarrassed at my inability to reply and my short-sightedness. The truth of his words permeates me albeit I refuse to accept that inevitability, a flurry of emotions skipping molto allegro inside me. "Farewell, Monsieur Sougo."

He bows graciously even when my steps carry me back into the shelf and towards my music box.

As I walk, the images of Sougo, André, and the sisters crawl through my mind, each marred by life and faring worse than me. The twins are melted into each other, poorly fixed and mangled. André is almost blind and dependent on spectacles, while Sougo is confined to his seat in the geode, with hands so maimed he can't even flip a book.

But me? *Me?* I'm just complaining about a ~~chip~~ speck of dust.

Their pain is greater, and my own is non-existent; not comparable to theirs at all. ~~That doesn't invalidate mine~~. I have no basis for comparing my stumbles to what they endure. What I felt was not pain or misery, just... a bother, a nuisance. Nothing that would entitle me to lament my woes. ~~But my back is sore and my legs are exhausted~~. No; I mustn't complain, I can't.

Protesting my own thoughts, I climb back into my music box with lumbering steps and I ease into the velvety compartment. The softness relaxes me, exhaustion takes over, and I doze off to the rhythm of unanswered, unyielding questions.

The days pass by in the same routine as before.

Three out of six the elven boy arrives at this cupboard, winds up my music box, and I dance for him. His approving hums ease me, his shocked gasps delight me, and his interest validates my ballet.

I stretch every afternoon and sleep every night instead of wandering, using the time to replenish myself—wandering around only yielded questions without answers, and I see no benefit in seeking more of those.

But... living like this is bland and unremarkable. A sequence as periodic as the tune in my box. It is my life, my ballet, and my music and so I dance, on and on, pushing the questions away with every leap.

Dawn glimmers through the room, and I awake and settle into a second position of arms and legs, bending glamorously. Today is the day. As per the schedule, the boy will come to me. To *me*! And I will dance for him!

Soon enough the door creaks ajar, and after slipping inside, he darts to my cupboard, wrestling with the latch. The glass doors rattle in place, the furniture protesting the abrupt motions —yet it doesn't scare me anymore. I have learned to keep my balance.

Heartbeats later, the glass doors unlock, opening and casting shimmers of light throughout my shelf. His embroidered sleeve shines upon me, walnut hand ~~roughly~~ winding up the music box while I steady myself.

I wait, counting the twists of that key, anticipation building as my need to dance grows. He releases the handle and the melody unfurls, and so I move, my ballet majestic as I piqué and sauté, visiting every angle of the dance floor and changing my motions to awe him again.

The music ends while I ease into an arabesque, my hand stretched elegantly to graze his finger as we so often do. A few last notes laze in an adagio and I open my eyes to gaze at him, coquettish and—

He snatches me. Fast and deft, jailing me inside his gigantic fist. My legs are spread and locked between his fingers, my arms crossed behind my head, contorted in pain. My hips hurt, and my shoulders strain. My chest heaves, and I can't breathe.

He moves, pulling me out from the shelf as a vacuum fills me, an abyss threatening beneath me.

"Why do you keep dancing?" The boy grits, rough and annoyed, his free hand poking a finger at my chin. "Why?" He repeats, pushing my head with each ~~dig~~ nudge.

~~"For you! For you!"~~ I shout in desperation, but only my thoughts bellow. Why is he doing this? He was ~~frowning~~ smiling at my ballet! What was my mistake? How did I fail? *"Tell me! I'll try harder! I will improve!"* My words die in my mind, restrained by the elves' magic, feeding my anguish and spiralling me into terror.

I scream, panicked and terrified of falling—but the holler only shouts within me; the tautness of my face is only my imagination. After all, I am still smiling for him.

He pokes me again, and I feel my lips curling into a grin because nothing else is allowed—I must please him, and a frown or a whince are not attractive. My hips hurt, my feet remain en pointe, and my arms stretch too delicately compared to his coarseness.

"You silly figurine," the boy grits ~~with hatred~~, emerald eyes glimmering gold with the morning's light. My hand curls gracefully to his, but he clicks his tongue. "Always pretending, always feigning."

~~"No, no! You wanted me to dance!"~~ No words, just a smile. *"I'm here to dance! For you! Always for you!"*

My shapeless arabesque, held in the air with my legs stuck at an angle, my hips shrieking in pain, my arms bent so ~~wrong~~ flexible.

He frowns at me, and my heart races. *"How did I fail you? Tell me, please. I'll learn and improve!"* ~~I beg and scream~~ I smile, coquettish and coy, needing his approval.

If he would tell me, I would dance just like he wants!

A voice rumbles through the corridor and the boy jerks, turning to the door. His grip relaxes, his fingers uncurl... and I *slip.*

My glossy ceramic slides easily, my legs disentangle from his fingers, and my hands lack the strength to grip.

There are no sounds, no voices, no colours.

I have no voice, no choice, no control.

There is a smile, and I keep it on while plunging towards the floor.

GO ON, DANCE

Reality slips away, suspending me in peril amidst a vacuum of nothing and everything. Thoughts, emotions, words, actions. They glissade off me, overriding me, overwhelming me. It is a hole, and I'm falling. It is a lie, and time is stopping.

Upended. Upturned.

It is an impossibility. A musical scale that exists below the bassiest note. An adagio that slows into grave, so solemn my hearts stills. The panic is unsettling, swirling, devouring. It is desolation, harvesting everything out of me. It is devastation, plunging me into oblivion as I fall. Fall. **Fall.**

That scream.

It shrills. Rippling the air in utmost silence, dove-like emeralds consumed into darkness, pure and undefiled. They watch me, shining in that walnut face, so absent and remote it seems another dimension of concern. And that mouth? Opulent and hiding beaming joy, now pursed into the thinnest thread (or threat?).

It's not his fault ~~(except it is)~~. He is not angry, but distressed ~~(but he is)~~. He cares, and is concerned ~~(he broke me)~~.

It hurts. *Everything* hurts.

Pain slithers from my back. It embraces and ravages me. It consumes and depletes, exhausting and squandering, draining and destroying. Everything and nothing—there is no goal, no pain greater than the one reflected in those emerald eyes ~~(It is anger, I see it)~~.

Stand. I **must** stand. I am NOT broken.

I imagine it, clear as the daylight. I stand and dance for him. ~~Those splinters are mine~~. I leap and pirouette. ~~This pain is not enough to complain~~.

My legs stumble and I lay down. ~~Broken~~. **Never!**

I rise, and I will dance!

My smile is in place, even when my shoulder shrieks. My eyelashes flip as I curl my legs. My pointe flats are splintered, but their box and platform remain intact. My knees creak, and ceramic rains ~~from~~ on me, sparkling with the morning's light.

I bloom, shredding those pieces, numb because there is only absolute nothingness. I plié, tiptoeing between the ceramic shards scattered around me. They mark a path on the enchanted wooden floor, a rhythm that I follow, flowing. There are no tears, just ear-splitting misery, an eminent smallness—yet I move, en avant.

For the boy. Onwards.

~~I'm broken, worthless~~. I keep dancing in the empty space of my nothingness, and dare a fouetté while bisque raindrops surround me, casting rainbows. I spin, leg whipping ~~the pain~~, my smile softening as I land and stretch my hand to him. My forefinger is up, the others poised.

"See? I danced for you! I will dance anywhere if that would please you!" My eyes plead to him, offering the words I cannot speak.

From here, the boy reaches the ceiling, his leather boots spread almost in second position. I cannot comprehend the gesture ~~of disgust~~ I see on his face. The perspective is impossible, the angle outrageous. His figure is gigantic, and I'm small, reaching up.

He squats, bending slowly, one hand grazing the floor with

its fingertips, the other hanging on his knee. Squinting, watching my extended, waiting hand.

"Please. I will improve my dancing," I beg, ~~mouthing silent words~~ battering my eyelashes. *"Don't throw me. I can still dance."*

I only manage to stretch further, smiling even when the ceramic shrieks and pain collides with my soul.

Another voice flares unintelligibly in the corridor and the boy jerks, looking over his shoulder with widened, panicked eyes. He snatches me again after a heartbeat, standing fast enough for the wooden floor to spin in meandering patterns.

"Please, don't-t hurt... me," I mumble, but my face doesn't move.

My lips *grin*—roguish, romantic. A perfect façade that endures even when he walks, shattering the scattered bisque flakes. He clutches me, and my arm prolongs behind my head, legs pressed by his fingers and scratching each other.

A door creaks open, and he lays me down on another wooden shelf. My arms relax, my feet persist en pointe, and ceramic rubs when my legs slide beside each other, thumping onto the wood. My head lolls to the side and I watch him dash to my original cupboard, fetching the music box while magic ignites from him.

Broken ceramic flows from the ground, lifting in a haze of bisque and light, some painted mauve, others with gold bits, a few with creamy decorations. They flow to me, adding ~~nothing~~, mending, *pretending*. That magic is inert, cursory, a polite disgrace, just like the boy's furrowed brows.

A tempo later, the music box tumbles near me, the dry thumps reverberating on the shelf's floor. Another tempo and the cabinet's door closes. Opaque, wooden-made. Clicking and locking itself.

Two more tempos and I sigh, certain that this is just a nightmare. ~~I will leap through the pain~~. I will sleep and wake up whole.

Just sleep, because this isn't real.
Rest, and find myself whole.
Sleep and dance again.
Just sleep, sleep, sleep.

"Wake up, lovely one." A contralto seeps through me, distant, melodious, thick, and inevitable. "Wake up. There is much to see."

"Hurt-ts. Every... where," I mumble, dizzy and numb. Everything hurts, tingling with strain, waving in a sea of agony.

"I know, little one." That voice softens, mild and fruity. "But you were courageous. You *danced*." The woman sighs, pained. "You may be in pain now, but there is plenty to live for."

Lazily, I open my eyes, taking in my surroundings. I'm still lying on the cabinet's shelf, on its floor, face turned towards the closed wooden doors. My right arm is stretched upwards—just like the boy left me—and my fingertips brush on gold filigree. Is that my music box? I can't move. My neck throbs, my chest heaves, and a thousand needles puncture my hips.

This shelf is dark and quiet. I can't hear anything except that voice.

"Where-am... I?" I stammer, exhausted but finally feeling my mouth shape the words again.

"On the closed cabinet of treasures," the contralto chuckles, so earthy and full, harmonious and calming. "You could come and meet me."

"Too... f-far," I whisper, hoarse. "I'm... exhausted."

"Then sleep and recover," she instructs, motherly and temperate. Who is this woman? "I will be here when you wake up."

Sleep. I'll sleep.

"Good morning, ballerina. The dawn shines bright." That contralto greets me, oh so motherly. "I was thinking of you."

"Who are... you?" I mumble, oh so dizzy. I'm still sprawled on that shelf. Nothing seems to have changed from the days before, and the pain rages through me.

"I'm Behati," she chuckles, fruity. "Sougo told me about you, child. You are Lyra, the ballerina." She lingers, but I remain silent, thinking. Sougo mentioned her before, implying she was wise. "How are you feeling?"

"T-tired. Exhausted," I hush, pained and weakened.

Behati doesn't answer, but I can hear her sing a lullaby for me. I lay motionless, breathing hard while wishing the dawn will put an end to this nightmare.

"Rise, little one. The morning is here and the clock will sing today," Behati welcomes me, soothing. "I was worried about you."

"Why do... you c-care?" I ask, almost sour. What compels her to speak to me? She would have come if she cared! But... her insistence and gentleness fill that vacuum inside me, highlighting my misery and adding more pain. "Why?"

"I don't need a reason," she explains, affable and without reproach. "I just wish to help."

I can't answer that, lacking the words and the concepts to shape what it ignites in me. ~~I'm not alone.~~ The boy left me; he abandoned me, but Behati... *cares* about me?

A headache sparkles at that thought, and I stretch mildly, slowly dozing off.

"Bonjour, ma belle. The day is pretty, and the air is pure today." Behati awakens me again, welcoming and caring. "I long to see you."

"It still hurts," I protest, feeble and trying to move. I'm feeling slightly better, but the noises chasing my movements feed the nightmares that threaten me at night. "Everything hurts."

I shuffle lazily, remaining on my back but finally bringing my hands to rest upon my chest, ceramic shrieking as I move. In the darkness, my fingers graze a few loose flakes and I just know those were once decorations on my clothing.

"I know, ma petite," Behati replies, her voice smothering part of my panic. "It may be scary, but you are strong, Lyra... and you are not alone."

She waits in silence, but I merely chuckle in my imagination, tapping my face and probing the smile, noticing a chip on the corner of my mouth. I had so many dreams, so many opportunities... but they are all gone now. All converted into nightmares. Breathing is painful, and being awake is just a mind-numbing experience. The clock ticks in the distance, the contralto hums a melody, and I hold on the verge of nightmares—those brought by slumber, those brought by wakefulness.

"Where... are you?" My question is hoarse, not as strained as before yet unlike my usual tone.

"On the same level, but to your left," she replies, so mellow and relaxed it is almost sing-song.

I look at the wooden ceiling and after a tempo I shiver in panic, my breathing raging in shame—that anyone would see me like this, so broken, so shattered, so splintered I cannot even move. I was locked in this closed cabinet to wear my shame in loneliness and not perturb the room's beauty.

"Calm, child. I respect your privacy," the contralto replies, as if aware of my misery. "I will be here whenever you want to visit me."

The silence stretches, undemanding. My body aches, pulsating with the minimal movement... but there is more to it. A misery that isn't physical, a vacuum I can't quite explain.

In the evening I stretch gently, laying on the floor and feeling my body ache. I wish to dance, to return to my life—to be myself. Perhaps tomorrow, when dawn comes, I will begin rehearsing.

"Child?" Behati calls, waking me up. "Dusk is almost here..." She trails off, the sting of worry darkening her voice. "Lyra? Wake up!"

Her concern startles me and I mumble words as incoherent as my thoughts. I muster my courage and move my arms, forcing the weight of my body to roll over my left side. Purple filters through the sliver between the cabinet's doors, and I use that shimmer as my guidance—to kneel, then to sit in a demi-plié, and finally stand.

I heave, ~~pained~~ exhausted, yet blossoming into standing. My music box looms from a distance and my gaze etches on its pristine ornaments while I plié ~~too slowly~~ into a first position, glancing at the looming darkness. My motions are stiff, my breathing is ragged, my humming interrupted by the cackling of ceramic.

It matters not. My body may be chipped, but I remember my purpose—to dance, to please the boy whose magic brought me alive.

"Lyra?" Behati asks so gently, her cadence in tandem with my hums. "Would you come and meet me?"

The echoes of her encouraging, soothing voice tease my response. "Yes..." I stumble, rolling my shoulders back and forth.

I do not need to think about this answer; I crave companionship, and she's been... motherly to me. "I'll come to you."

My first steps are gentle, yet I stumble en avant—mincing, sneaking, wondering what the dust is. ~~Mine, all mine~~. Rims of dusk seep through the cracks in the doors, reflecting on gemstones scattered in this place. There is a ring, and I advance past it. A crystal figurine, earrings dangling with magic, and a miniature amethyst-made rabbit.

A few steps ahead, a box of gold filigree ripples like stars of bronze and ruby in the night—gorgeous and elaborate, and I approach it with hands poised in an adage. After uncountable tiptoes, my fingers graze the soft rim and my ceramic clings to it as I reach the edge and peer inside.

The box's entrance is shaped like a golden arch, the surroundings graceful like an opulent theatre stage but illuminated from the back with miniature dragonflies. They shimmer, tracing patterns in the air while swirling around the woman dancing in the middle.

Behati is carved from sard—translucent chalcedony, reddish-brown and deep—and dressed in a gown threaded from pure gold. The jewellery she wears is rich and elaborate, earrings and necklace each brimming with a ruby as carmine as her pout. Her eyes are nacre-made, opalescent yet kind, and her long black curls bounce like a cloak while she waltzes, adding rhythm to the imaginary music she's dancing to.

"You are... g-gorgeous," I mumble, humbled by her sheer flawlessness.

"And you are perfect, Lyra." She smiles so honestly and truthful I *almost* believe her. My mouth falls agape, fractures shrieking, yet her nacre eyes look right through me. "I'm grateful that you came."

I gape, unsure what to say. ~~I'm broken and worthless, abandoned in this dark cabinet~~. "Why?" A mumble, delayed and hiding my bewilderment under a pleased smile. **"Why?"** Demanding; heart shattered.

Behati approaches me, towering a head taller than me. "Because I wanted to do this…"

Her fingers thread through my chin, caressing my cheek, and curling around me. A hug. So protective, so understanding. One arm across my shoulders, the other hand patting my updo.

I stand there, motionless. Thoughtless, speechless. Warmth bathes me, careful and affectionate.

"You are in pain, and it is overwhelming," Behati whispers, chin resting atop my head. "It will be challenging from now on, but you are not alone."

My throat is tense, my tears not flowing. The ~~fractures~~ lines criss-crossing my body stir while dust falls slightly ~~from~~ around me. The magic keeps me whole ~~but broken~~, some fragments wishing to believe in Behati, the others dreading the hope she brings.

"Am… not?" My words come loose like a breath of air, a gush of wind, a silent note that she still catches.

"I'm here. Sougo and André as well. We are here whenever you need us." She mends something invisible within me, and if it is a lie, it is one I'll gladly believe—at least for now.

Behati embraces me still through the night, shielding me from reality. It's late when she walks me across the shelf, her hair bobbing behind us, the silence a respectful cadence.

She holds my hand as I climb into my music box, and she guides me to my sleeping compartment with that motherly care that mends every ~~flaw~~ unpleasant thought. With her help, I slide into it, the velvety, cushiony pillows luring me into a slumber.

Mildly awake, I feel her cheek pressing into my ~~cracked~~ forehead. "You are flawless, little ballerina."

Tonight, I dream of an opera. They are cheering for me.

The dawn filters through the cabinet's closed door, rimming it with bronze and gold. The shine almost blinds me, but as I yawn and stretch, the shrieks of my ~~fractures~~ lines become less distressing. Slowly, I rise from the sleeping compartment, rolling my shoulders and beginning my elongation.

Gentle tendus at first, testing my balance and moving en arrière and derrière. It requires a shamefully long moment, but I ease into splits, elongating until my legs are entirely straight and my back doesn't ache—there is a nuisance, but nothing else.

How many days have passed? I wonder, craning my neck to stretch it. It's been days or weeks, and I've not heard from the boy. How many days did I lay on the shelf's ground? Reality is slipping away from me like a distant repetition, a blend of mornings, afternoons, and nights, so amalgamated there is no beginning or end.

Twirling, I test a port de bras, my arms extended into the side, unfurling like a blossoming flower. Smiling—truthful, for once—I slowly lower into a grand plié, rising with control to—

The room's door creaks open, its latch bouncing noisily. It startles me into a soft relevé, my heart pounding alongside the boy's stumbling steps.

Joy fills me, brightening the darkness of that awful cabinet. He came for me! I knew it! I knew this was only another small sanction! After all, it was my fault since I couldn't hold on to his fingers.

Excited and merry, I perk in the centre of my dance floor, standing in fourth position and ready to move as soon as he opens these doors and winds up my music box.

One heartbeat passes with papery noises, another with giggles and gasps—but the footsteps don't approach this enclosed cupboard. What is he trifling with?

Inquisitive ~~and concerned~~, I ease my pose and descend the box's staircase, tiptoeing towards the edge between both doors to peer into the room's table.

The elven boy is alone; his amethyst velvet coat shining with silver embroidery, his long black braids knotted elegantly. He leans into my ~~former~~ rightful cupboard across the room, and despair silences me when a new music box shines brightly, set in *my* place.

Emptiness tickles down my shoulders, a vacuum as dark as this cabinet enclosing my heart.

The boy replaced me. Forgot me. Dumped me because I'm broken. Hid me from sight and found a stunning figurine to dance for him. Am I so disgusting? So cracked and fissured he can't withstand my appearance? Do I look worse than the sisters? Am I as motionless as Sougo?

A handle chafes, rolling and thumping while music blossoms, stately and elegant. The magic swirls from the boy, sparkling like golden starlight, spiralling and vibrating as if directing an orchestra—and the figure atop that box unfurls, saluting and moving en avant, tiptoeing around their dance floor.

It is a man, a danseur, with short caramel hair and a military jacket. His legs are toned, and his grand battements are perfectly controlled, impressive, and gentlemanly done.

I retreat, gasping and panting, patting my face to corroborate I am still smiling. Then, I prod my updo and romantic tutu and chase my distress across the shelf and up the stairs of my box. The dancing area awaits me, lonely and discarded ~~like myself~~ but I bow to the darkness of this cabinet.

There is music, and I will *dance*.

My ballet flows unhindered as I move en avant. I plié and pirouette and, at the right moment, swirl in so many fouettés the number is lost to me. My grand jeté is exquisite, unblemished and immaculate, so faultless that ~~ceramic~~ starlight rains upon me. I land gracefully, pirouetting before the music ends.

The boy claps for me ~~(he isn't)~~ and I révérence. He will come to me ~~(he won't)~~, I know it. He misses me ~~(he forgot me)~~ so much he just bought me a dancing partner ~~(he replaced me)~~.

He laughs and claps ~~but not~~ to my dance; that sound is comforting ~~painful~~, but it is all I have left besides the ballet. All that I *deserve* after so many failures.

Empty and devoid of feelings, I stand on the dance floor while the afternoon fades away, the darkness enduring until the night rumbles stormy and raging.

It thunders across the room, as wild as motionless and shocked as I am.

It quiets long after, pouring and dropping at the same rhythm as my heart cries in silence.

A new sunrise blossoms in a silvery haze.

I wait for hours in a relevé, and when ~~his~~ my box plays loudly and magically, I dance with my eyes closed, letting the melody flow through me.

The next day is similar, except the dawn is gold and I plié and begin in fifth position, dancing when a melody flows.

On the following one, I commence in fourth position, and after that, in an arabesque.

Between that cadence of silence and music, the days fade away again. I dance, ~~he dances~~, over and over. From an arabesque to a spin, whipping my ~~pain~~ leg, traversing the penumbra because only the music guides me.

Did I please the boy? No; perhaps my jeté wasn't adequate, or my split was not straight enough.

It doesn't matter what I do; the elven boy won't notice me.

Not anymore.

I keep dancing ~~and weeping~~, chasing the music. Day after day, whenever I hear it and when I don't. It is all that matters; my ballet is all I have. I dance through the days, even when all melodies fade. Humming and singing about pretty flowers and book stories. Moving and leaping, pirouetting while smiling.

Always.

Always, even when my body spills dust from its ~~fractures~~ lines. Whatever happens, I keep twirling, soaring, and bowing because that is the only thing ~~I'm good at~~ I have left.

The mirror on my music box doesn't reflect me on this endless night, but my smile remains as my ballet grows stronger. The notes flow through me. The melody becomes me, and my body sways alongside its cadence.

Steps echo somewhere, and I imagine the boy skipping in awe at me. Light bathes me and I spin in a double tour en l'air because if that danseur can, I will as well. A gasp resonates near while I turn in the air, landing correctly and following with an arabesque.

My splits are superb, my rhythm is synchronised, and my stardust shines beautifully as I stabilise into a grand adage. The music unfurls, louder and powerful while the light flourishes into an eclipse, a trim of bronze embracing me from afar.

The ballet is part of me; it *is* me, and my placement is perfect.

I hop and leap in pas d'élévation, jumping in entrechat and landing in fifth position, my feet rapidly crossing. I pirouette again and when the tune fades I révérence.

Only then I understand.

My music box was playing. *My* box, *my* music.

I look around and the boy is here, grinning with ~~repulsion~~

awe while holding the edge of the cabinet's open doors. The silk of his aquamarine coat diffusing the light, swivelling and shushing as he crouches with hands on knees to align with my shelf. His emerald eyes are shocked, opulent lips gawking.

I smile gently, settling into arabesque penchée and holding the split flawlessly straight while I offer my hand to him—forefinger up as we used to do.

"I can still dance for you." The words only resonate in my mind while I grin, poised and coy. Romantic. *"Do you like me?"* ~~Am I enough again?~~

The boy moves slowly, looking over his shoulder before returning to me. He lifts me with care, fingers curling around my torso and back. The other hand wrestles with the music box, opening the sleeping compartment before shoving me in. Velvet embraces me as my heart sprints prestissimo, bumping and throbbing, flooding me with anguish so profound it stalls my mind into a vacuum.

Am I that hideous that he'll hide me? Is this dark cabinet not enough? Will he trash me?

"Why!? I danced! I danced for you!!" I scream, but the words don't come.

The compartment tucks closed and darkness embraces me.

Footfalls. The boy's. Rhythmical, known.

My legs are crossed and en pointe once more, my arms stretched over my torso. A sweet, earthy scent seeps inside.

"What was my mistake? What did I do wrong?" I plead, begging mutedly within this ~~cage~~ compartment. If he'd tell me, I'd learn and never fail again!

After an eternity, the box settles with another thump. Something rolls, and music begins; distant, muted. The ~~cage~~ compartment slides open, and light blinds me for a tempo before his hand curls around my entire torso and halts.

My ankle is stuck between the velvet drapes.

The boy jerks me up, and my foot unlocks with an explosion of needles, traversing upwards and rippling into my calf.

He drops me onto the dance floor, and I disguise my stumbles with a balancé sideways—like a waltz, tiptoeing as a pendulum. From there, I attempt a petit battement with small kicks from one side of the ankle to the other, and brisé. The needles on my ankle add to the tempo, the pounding on my calf is a drum, and the creaks are bells on the music.

My dance is empty, void, and hollow like my fall, desolated and deserted as my heart.

Vacant like the boy's eyes.

He nods at me when the melody ends, irking an inquisitive eyebrow before backtracking and closing the glass-made doors of *my* cupboard. From that vantage point, the elf glimpses at the closed cabinet on the far wall, tilts his head, and retreats out of the room.

The door closes with a shriek and I sigh, exhausted, falling to my knees, caught by my reflection.

Those lines on my face are *nothing*. The throbbing in my ankle is a metric. The grains flowing around me are stardust.

I have no reason to complain—the boy returned me to my cupboard, to a level higher than before, and thus I will dance.

Whatever happens, I will dance.

GILDED CAGE

The dawn rises, the dusk flares purple, and the night quiets into stretches and tendus, on the shelf's floor or atop my music box.

Some nights find me hidden in the velvet container, so dreamless and heavy I wake up without knowing what happened. In others, I stare at this figure I've become while hideously enthralled by the reflection.

There are lines on my face where the glazing used to be smooth. There are chips in my updo where gold trims curled opulent. My legs feel dry and rough instead of polished; sometimes they squeak, and other times shriek.

The truth is irrevocable.

I'm fractured, broken. *Worthless.*

I stretch an arm, and the joint screeches, a nuisance spreading through my shoulders until it eases up. I pose them in fifth position, both up and barely brushing. My neck stirs, and some knots unwind, rippling through until they fade. That didn't happen before, and I can't quite ignore that.

I split my legs, the left at the front while easing myself down... but there is a speck of uncomfortable tension, a tautness, a weariness to move. I exhale, bending and pushing my stiff arms; they are unreal, unwelcome.

Through the days a part of myself fades away and what I am becoming, this cracked self, is no longer recognisable.

How long has it been since the boy brought me back to this cupboard? Months? *Years?*

He is unpredictable, sometimes gentle as if I were crystal-made, others rough and angry, yanking and poking me. It is all my fault, albeit the reason escapes me.

Days pass and I dance when he comes, with the music from my box and at any tune streaming around. I dance when he smiles or frowns, and even when he ~~shouts angrily~~ sings loudly alongside the tune.

By night I am swarmed by the exhaustion of standing on my tiptoes the entire day, dancing while the boy plays with the box's dainty key.

There is always a ~~frown~~ smile on his face, mouth agape in awe ~~grimacing in displeasure~~.

Tonight I bend, back arching slowly towards the side, tired calves gradually giving in until my fingers reach the pointe flats. I stand once my body eases into the position, angling to the floor and letting the dust fall through.

From this angle, and with the shadows half bathing my face, I *almost* look like myself. Smooth, perfect, *healthy*.

I smile as a memory returns to me like a forgotten song—and it is truthful. Irrevocably so. Sougo said life marks us all, and it brandished me, indeed. Back then I was aloof, silly. *Young.* I saw the sisters and was repulsed by them, thinking that life wouldn't fracture me... as if I were special. Yet now I'm spilling dust while unable to cry, gold filigree abraded into dullness.

Another memory returns, spoken in Behati's contralto—yet it is a lie, a gruesome lie. She said I was flawless, and the echoes of her voice disarm me into sobbing because the mirror of my box shows the truth, and only the truth.

A fissured figurine that shouldn't be dancing.

But if I don't, what do I have left?

Frustrating as it is, the answer is simple. I can't stop since there is nothing else in my life other than the ballet. This is all my fault; I should have done better. I am a poor ballerina, unfit for my only purpose and goal.

Carefully, I steady with hands on knees, on hips, and on the sides, balancing up. My ceramic screeches and, for a nervous exhalation, I think I'll shatter again... but I endure, held together with magic unknown to me—the boy's, always and forever.

His memory is bitter, worry adding to my concerns. He brought me here, infused me with life. His sadness is due to my fractures and I can't bear the weight of that shame.

I sigh, exhausted and embarrassed. Ashamed of what I'm becoming and afraid of my inability.

It is late, and the night's silence slips past, threatening to send me into the darkest sleep where my well-deserved misery lives.

It is late when a few voices float back to me. Even through my stupor, I've learned a few things by idly eavesdropping. The danseur was named Dorian, and his voice is calm and collected, steady and graceful.

Part of me wants to meet him, but there are two ideas, equally truthful and opposed, conflictive but equivalent—jealousy and something unrecognisable, undefinable. They surround me as I sit on the velvety sleeping compartment, legs stretched as the fluffiness relaxes me.

Oh, how I crave to feel perfect again! So flawless and elegant! How I wish to mend these fractures!

I am the broken one now, undeserving of this world of beauty... yet somehow, I am not damaged enough. I can walk and dance when Sougo is stuck in his chair, when André can't read without his glasses, and the twins are melded together.

My face frowns in my imagination, the mirror showcasing my coy smile.

I should go on. Keep dancing.

My exhaustion is not enough. My darkness is not crippling enough. My fractures are not deep enough.

So I sit in my music box, back turned to the mirrored lid, eyes averting the dance floor while the night fades away again.

Day after day, the boy comes and spins the music box.

I dance to its tune, always, and without understanding why sometimes he shouts at me, while in others he caresses my head. I cried the last time he did that, and my smile was so lovely that he grabbed me and couldn't stop ~~poking~~ thumping it... and perhaps, he chipped it a bit more.

Tempos after dusk, I'm sitting on my dance floor, legs stretched before me. The clock taps rhythmically and loud, having bothered me since the boy upgraded me to this higher shelf. It's metrical and measured, swirling and tapping four times, shushing and tapping four more.

A soprano's voice comes from the same direction; chiming but delightful, sometimes humming a tune, others simply talking about whatever she's working with. She sounds affable enough but *nothing* like Behati; this woman is always cheerful, loud, and excitable—as if the clock would rush her into singing prestissimo.

Her energy intrigues me beyond reason, and after a few heartbeats my need to meet her has grown to occupy all my thoughts. I'm seeking something without knowing what it is, and she's unwillingly become a candidate to offer it—company, or perhaps soothing words.

Twirling into a stand, I stretch with a few tendus while wondering how long it's been since I spoke to another statuette. Behati was the last... but that entire season is a blur in my mind.

Flickering those dark moments away, I finish my elongations and pat my petal-like peplum to ensure the chips aren't flaking more than usual. Mildly pleased, I prod my updo; it's different now, rough in parts when before the glazing was smooth and flawless. That realisation distresses me and, unknowingly, I face the mirror—but the moonlight softens my reflection, encouraging me enough to descend from my box.

Once on the floor I move delicately, skulking en pointe, cautious and fearing both disturbing this quietude or enhancing my fractures. This level is cluttered with trinkets, closed boxes, earrings and jewels displayed inside crystal cases, their trail leading me to my destination—a box made of the cupboard's wood. It seems to be part of it, the shelf itself twisting to create a path into the roombox's entrance.

"Who roams there?" The soprano enquires, dubious. Metal clatters and beads clang together like a tool rolling over a table. "Come! Please!" Her voice chirps, trebling before whispering softly and embarrassed. "I'm bored and need another hand to hold the gears. *Je vous en prie!*"

The question takes me aback, and I look at the box while

wondering whatever gears she's speaking of. The clock echoes closer than before, but its ticking comes from above, not from ahead.

"Are you... well?" I ask, confident in my pronunciation but not daring a step forward. "What happened?"

The soprano groans, and more metal clatters. "The clock's gears, little one," she explains, fingers tapping wood. "Would you help? I should have asked for assistance, but, mon dieu, the Warlock is with Behati again!"

That nickname startles me, and I chuckle while thinking of André; he mentioned some figurines called him names. Regardless, her effusive behaviour entices me, and I tiptoe carefully en avant, moving alongside the box's edge to peer inside.

Her place is overflown with the haze of spells, cobalt magic swirling in the back through a portal. The other walls are ridden with gears and clocks, gemstones and levers, all twirling and pulling, tickling and cackling in a rhythmical concoction that marks the tempo with singular precision.

The soprano—carved from ivory—sits in the middle, her long, wavy hair made of the thinnest copper. It flows with magic, connecting gems and gears to the mechanism on the walls. Her right arm is stretched into the inside of that magical portal, her slender fingers manipulating something but blurred by the spell. The other arm bends at the elbow, holding a wooden piece entangled with her hair and sparkling as if malfunctioning.

She is wearing a metal-made bustier, and her skirt lies low on her navel. Its layers of silk blend into copper and gold foil, opening... into a wooden cabinet that sprouts from the room's centre, merging with her hips.

I blink twice, meeting her gaze and understanding.

This soprano is not a figurine living inside the clock. She *is* the clock.

J.a.BUVA
2023

"Little one?" The clock-lady calls, eyes made of shungite and shimmering black, reflecting that enchanted storm. "Will you fetch that gear for me?" She says, her carmine pout beckoning to a little piece near my damaged pointe flats.

Bewilderment overtakes me as I stare at the part, copper and shimmering with magic. Then, I glance at her arm stuck in that magical storm, at her missing legs and the piece again—and nod, bending elegantly to pick it up and stroll towards her.

"I'm... Lyra," I offer, proffering the contraption with both hands.

"Margot, the clock master," she hushes me, humming a crescendo and lifting the gear with her voice alone. It hovers to join that mass of copper hair, wood, and metal pieces she's holding with her left hand. "Thank you, little ballerina."

Hesitating, I révérence while barely mumbling, "Y-you're w-welcome." Stammered and childish, the curt statement a poor façade to the many doubts cavorting in my mind.

Margot chuckles, copper hair sparkling while dots of light traverse it back and forth. "Oh, you have questions shimmering in your eyes!" She laughs, and it is *contagious*. She is one of a kind, elegant but jovial, unafraid of being herself, yet regal at the same time. "Ask, ma chérie. Sougo told me you were curious!"

I blush, embarrassed to be read so accurately while pretending that the dust and creaks come from the swirling magic and not me. The portal behind her whooshes loudly and the clock above us strikes one—half an hour, clearly controlled by this woman.

"What... are you holding?" I seize the moment, clasping my hands near my navel and glancing towards the device Margot is clutching.

"A cross-world lever," she states nonchalantly, as if the word meant anything to me. After blinking impassively, her mouth shapes into a ruby circle, and her ivory cheeks blush. "You see, each part of this world has a different hour. We are at night, but those in Ierlei are welcoming the dawn." Margot sings, and the device floats into the magic storm, landing in her hand inside it. "Everything breaks after a while, and this needed maintenance. My job is to keep this clock, well... *clocking!*"

"Did you f-fix it?" I wonder, intrigued while tiptoeing closer to see. "Does it work now?"

"Thanks to you," Margot chuckles, her fingers working deftly into the magic portal without her even looking at it. The device's copper hairs extend, intertwining around her own and shirring into life—and she laughs again, pleased. "Done! Et quelle solution splendide!"

I chuckle at her enthusiasm, enthralled by whatever work she does here. The silence extends, perturbed by the clicking and ticking of gears, and I finally notice a truth—the walls and ceiling are covered with mechanisms, the portal is positioned at hands' reach, and the clock seemingly built around Margot.

As if she couldn't do anything but keep it working, her life and purpose defined by this gigantic contraption... almost as ballet has defined me.

My lips part, tremulous, a question building until I stammer, "Is this c-clock... a big r-responsibility?" My lips quiver into a smile, the spell restricting my emotions while I think of the correct words. "A burden? Too much?"

Margot frowns for a heartbeat. "It certainly was for a while! Things, passions, and desires aren't static, ma chérie." Lingering, she hums until a small gear hovers atop her fingertips, pirouetting by sheer will. "Some days, I feel so powerful I could spin all the clocks in the world with a flick of my fingers. But others? Oh là là! Sometimes I can barely keep *this* clock ticking on time!" Her smile smooths, and she drops another gear; it vanishes into thin air. "It's natural, Lyra. It is *life*, and the best thing you can do is admit that we are as fluctuating as the wind itself."

Bewildered, I tiptoe around the entrance, glancing at the clock while wondering how she can withstand so much responsibility. Before she spoke of acceptance and resilience, yet I can imagine there is more—there would be, at least for me. Knowing her motivations awakens my curiosity... but knowing why she stays intrigues me more.

Perhaps, through her, I can find my own reasons. It is a vague hope, yet one worth pursuing.

"But d-did you ever wish t-to leave?" I whisper, blushing instantly and lowering my gaze in shame. "In those d-days, I mean. W-when you're t-tired."

"Decades ago, when newly crafted, I certainly wished to leave... but something changed with the pass of time, and I spent decades working only on this." Margot tilts her head, removing her hand from the magic portal, and intertwining both near her navel. "There is much more to life than a simple task, ma chérie, and when I realised that, I began performing duets with Sougo or singing with Behati when she came. André helped me connect this—" She points to a small handle on the leftmost wall. "—to his brother's library nook, and we began talking. Le Professeur's conversations are never boring!"

"That's... resourceful," I comment, watching the handle and wondering whether I could have the same strength were I in her position. My situation is far less complex, yet I can barely endure it.

"Do you want to know how I did it?" Margot interrupts my thoughts, tittering. Her eyes narrow curiously, voice thinning into a mischievous whisper. "I had help," she confesses, rolling a hand as if to dismiss her past self. "I rejected it a few times, but when I accepted it, my world *changed*."

I dare a few steps onward, hands clasping near my chest. "What changed?" I ask her, yearning to learn from her wisdom. Sougo was correct in praising her.

Margot doesn't answer immediately, and her features soften in that in-between. Her dark eyes shimmer peacefully—knowing, oh so knowing—and her hair sparkles with magic.

"*I* changed, ma chérie," she whispers after a long while, speaking calmly as if her answer were an obvious truth. "You see Lyra, many times I rejected any help because I believed it would make me *less*—that relying on someone else, even for the briefest of moments, would brand me incapable for as long as magic animates me... but it is not true." Margot smiles at me before beckoning at the magical portal. "On those occasions, I am not less apt at handling this clock than I am now."

A moment passes in silence, the ticking like a metronome that refuses to stop yet endures, ignored, in hopes someone would waltz at its tune. The clicking grows louder in this impasse, my feelings stacking unyielding with each creaking noise.

This woman's resilience is even greater than Sougo's, and her gentleness is only comparable to Behati's. More cheerful than André, and certainly wiser than I could ever be. In turn... here I am, struggling with a few fractures, staining everything with my dust instead of carrying on like them.

"Lyra?" Margot asks, so gentle and lovely. "It's late, and you must rest. The elves may come in the morning."

I want to frown but simply tilt my head, confused by the carefulness and softness of her tone—gentle, as if caring. She is not incorrect; I am depleted and yearn to sleep.

"Thank you, Madame Margot." I curtsey, letting the magic smile for me; it helps me to hide the maelstrom of incoherence that assails me.

I want to understand her words, but cannot comprehend their meaning—as if my darkness would clutch me because it's simpler to stay than force a way out. She hums musically and dips her head, and I turn around to amble away from her clock.

Is the ballet a burden to me? I wonder, tiptoeing en avant towards my music box. My routine felt boring once, yet now I long for that simplicity, too aware it'll never come back. It was so easy back then, so simple! I was so innocent, so naïve!

Annoyed, I run and leap into a grand jeté, pirouetting and flowing, landing with grace and curling into an arabesque.

My fractures are nothing compared to the others' ailments. Once, I felt ashamed for the help received—refusing André's offer to wind up my box's key, embarrassed for yearning for another of Behati's hugs. But as I twirl, pirouetting in place, I think of Sougo and his thoughts about life, his peaceful tenor bringing an understanding long forbidden.

I am *not* like them. I am not strong, not marred enough, not wise enough.

That certainty ~~enrages~~ empowers me and I advance on a brisé because otherwise, I will plunge into nothingness, losing my identity. Reaching the music box, I climb into the dancing area and begin a petit battement, followed by a développé, bending my knees first during the lift and extending them straight.

"Your technique is superb." Someone says, charming and alluring, pleasant and magnetising. Honest? ~~Mocking~~. Truthful? ~~Lying; perfectly so~~.

I spin, shocked. I recognise that voice, even if I only heard it from afar. It's Dorian's, so controlled it reduces me to a shocked gasp.

My position breaks at the interjection, and I take a few steps en derrière, seeking the shadows to hide my fractures. Where is my ballerina's restraint? My curated mask flakes at his gesture, yet a smile replaces my gawking.

He curtsies to me, perhaps oblivious to my flaws, while stepping into the penumbra. The moonlight illuminates his features, and his image is humbling—handsome, ~~unblemished~~ striking and porcelain-made, with a perfectly defined jaw and a gait attuned and curated.

Something coils in my stomach at his sight, and a dizziness arises after I notice his flawless smoothness.

Envy.

Jealousy because I was once so impeccable, so unmarred. Before, my dance was candid, but now it is impelled. ~~Coerced~~. He pities me, and his amiable compassion is harsher than dancing en pointe barefooted.

"I'm Dorian. Pleased to meet you," he greets me, bowing with a hand across his chest, slender pale fingers clinking against the porcelain outfit. "Please, forgive me. I should've introduced myself before."

"You are forgiven," I answer curtly, averting my head.

He was brought here to replace me, and I don't want a friendship or his condolences. I'm not here to make him feel better about his wholeness. After all, the elven boy now plays with his music box more than with mine.

Dorian grins, elegant, so obnoxiously alluring I am reminded of the dust spilling whenever I smile, or the fissures slivering my features with fine lines—and my hesitation sours his gesture. He wavers, and panic floods me in the silence surrounding us— incoherent and puzzling but also reasonable and rational.

I want him to stay and talk to me ~~(as a punishment, a reminder of my brokenness)~~, but I also want him to leave because loneliness is simpler. That inner dissonance stalls me, my feelings battling in a quiet fugue while I stay silent—until, amidst that disharmony, a realisation settles in. Dorian has only been here for a while, yet his speech is fully developed... as if he'd never had that impediment at all. Meanwhile, I had to rehearse and still stammer like a fool.

"I..." Dorian lingers, hesitating and speaking timidly. "I was thinking we could talk since you are a ballerina..." A pause, a step onwards, head tilting to look up at me on my dance floor. He grins again, his stance so effortless and sincere. ~~So mocking and ridiculing~~.

"Talk?" I feign ignorance, placing a hand on my heart because it aches with misery ~~(but Dorian can't stay, he can't)~~. "I must rest."

Dorian gapes, fighting back a smile while his brows arch but ease, seemingly restricted by the same spell that controls me—yet that awareness isn't enough to elicit my empathy. This danseur is faultless and polished, fracture-less and smooth. I have no reason to pity him, just to envy him.

"I understand," he whispers after his struggle ends, sombre. "But before I leave... please know that you can call me. The Warlock gave me this..." He kneels, placing a small gemstone on the floor. It shimmers cobalt, perfectly facetted. "If either of us taps it, the other will know. I just—" Dorian stutters, almost ~~mocking~~ concerned, curious perhaps. "I'd love to talk to you more."

I do not approach, instead clasping my hands and shielding myself with the shadows—the moonlight is blissfully gentler than the sunlight, yet I cannot risk it. He can't see how I look.

The silence stretches again, taut like the harmonics of a tense string, and Dorian retreats a few steps back. "You haven't told me your name."

My lips purse or pout, hiding my tremors. He is so kind ~~fake~~, so deceitful. Yet I... don't really know what else to do but oblige.

"Lyra," I bow gently, still eyeing that cobalt. "Sleep well, Dorian."

He révérences, accepting my dismissal and departing almost too hastily. I watch him walk, my gaze following his every step until he vanishes through some distant books—and then I leap through the music box, descending its steps, rounding on the shelf, and reaching for the gemstone.

It glimmers, pulsating, a cloud of magic vibrating inside it.

I blush, grinning instead of grimacing in distress, once again glancing at the path he followed. ~~He was mocking me~~. Perhaps one day I will call him... or maybe I will forget him. ~~He was toying with me; he didn't mean it.~~ I am not worthy for someone like him. ~~I am! I am!~~

Returning to my music box, I stuff the little gemstone

beneath the velvet in the sleeping compartment, cover it with the fabric, and finally sleep.

The days fall back into a routine.

Dance one day, hear Dorian dance on another. The mother comes very occasionally, always stopping in the sisters' miniature room first (oh, how I envy them!). When she speaks to me, her words blur into lies.

The boy regularly plays with my box. Sometimes, he gasps in awe at me; others, he yanks me. It's always the same, nonsensical and impossible to understand. He's gentle when the mother is here, but when alone he speaks the truth—I am broken, fractured, fissured, spilling dust and obstructing the shelf.

I dance nonetheless.

I dance and fouetté, swirling and leaping into a grand jeté. I tiptoe in blissé or waltz sideways, teasing or romantic, however the music flows within me.

Yet when it stops, my forefinger always stretches after my grand adage, challenging him. The elven boy loved this once, and he does so when the mother is here—but now, it means something more to me. Something I cannot quite decipher.

The boy pokes me once, yet my balance stands.

He bows to me another day, and I smile, but he pushes my music box the following morning, and I stumble to the dance floor. New cracks emerge while others deepen, and some chips grow rougher—but I stand up and continue my ballet.

Always, I dance.

My ceramic may be shredding away from me, but I dance with a smile on my lips and the melody coursing through my body. But even then, with every tempo and every leap, I ponder the same, poignant question.

Why do I keep dancing?

BROKEN HEART

I was foolish once, and that truth is indisputable. I was entitled and thought that dancing, my only ~~purpose~~ job, was tedious... just to realise it was all I had. All I *am*.

There is no 'me' without the ballet. Thus my legs carry me through the days and into meaningless pirouettes, brisès, and arabesques.

The days blend into each other, hopping between oblivion and awareness. I forget about the dust spilling from my fractures or the chips near my smile where the boy pokes me. One fissure or another, I've lost count of them all; they now traverse my legs like cobwebs.

Dawn awakens and here I stand again, my dance floor reflecting my silhouette, half-shadowed by the golden light that seeps into the room. A soft breeze comes from the window, and the curtains flutter as delicate as my brisé—the music is blossoming, and my ballet unfurling alongside it.

The boy watches me from afar, hands clasped behind his back, lips pressed to a dot as he hums to the tune on Dorian's box.

My legs carry me through this foreign music, and I swirl and sway, spinning until the colours blur and the gold filigree of this room of beauty becomes a fuzzy glimmer. The melody slows into an adage and I land on an arabesque, hand poised in an offer, a gentle smile adorning my fractured face. My heart races prestissimo at twice the tempo I have been dancing to, while my thoughts scatter, unable to concentrate on anything except my own body.

~~It isn't pain~~. I should be able to carry on, to dance without complaints—but I can't, so weak that I am, so flawed and broken, so unworthy of my place in this cupboard.

Distress opens my eyes—and I see the boy ignoring my efforts, leaning into Dorian's level to speak words of blurred sounds.

How I wish the boy would keep visiting as the mother does with the sisters! How I wish he would love me, as she loves the twins or André! How I envy Sougo who she visits so often, talking to him and bringing him new incense.

My questions absorb me, melting me into a soft relevé as the morning blends into stretches. The afternoon vanishes in a few tendus, and the night finds me standing on my box, ignoring that irreverent mirror.

Suddenly, the shelf's wood ripples with the sounds of prudent steps, and I spin towards them—the motion reigniting the sharpness that punctuates my lower back. I swallow a gasp, covering my mouth with my hand while retreating into the shadows. My heart skips a few beats, and I move further again, dreading those footfalls as they traverse the shelf. After a few tempos, Dorian emerges from between some books and stops near my music box, bowing to me.

I answer minutely, barely dipping my head. It's been days since he gave me that cobalt, and I've never used it... yet, until now, he had respected my choice, staying away from this level.

But Dorian ignores my distress, instead grinning roguishly. "This morning I felt you dancing alongside me. I... imagined it was a duet and must confess—" He glances at the box's steps, his intent clear albeit he does not move. "—I wished it was."

My mouth parts, speechless yet emotionless.

Is he offering me to dance with him? *Me?* It must be a sham; a poorly made jest, a farce as large as myself. Why would he do this? I must be mistaken; probably confused by a language I still don't master. It is impossible he'd wanted to dance with me! Evidently, he came to deride me—but no. The boy's ~~un~~expected actions are enough. I don't need this.

As my silence stretches, Dorian's face contorts, his porcelain countenance struggling against the spell. He probably wants to scorn me, but when he wins the battle against the limited gestures, his features are impassive—but his eyes... is that pain?

"Forgive me," he says, that tenor of his quivering into a muted hush. "I didn't intend to give offence. For what is worth, I... meant it."

"No offense taken," I answer without thinking. A storm of unlabelled, unrecognised emotions assails me like a conjunction of instruments poorly attuned to each other. "I wish to have seen you dance. The glass doors reflect little."

Dorian perks up, his countenance illuminating. "I could ask the Warlock for a mirror. Do you know him?"

I dip my head in polite agreement. "I do. He helped me once," I offer, my treacherous feet carrying me towards the music box's staircase. "André is... exuberant."

The danseur follows along, eyes twinkling as I descend yet only daring a few steps closer.

"You have a marvellous view," he comments once I'm on the shelf's wooden floor, beckoning at the room beyond. "I am two levels down, and not even the moonlight flickers the same."

I nod clumsily, clasping my hands to hide my unwarranted

shivers. This turn of the conversation startles me, and my countenance stills because of the sheer oddity of his comment. The moment stretches, and I blink in confusion, pondering whether I'm missing any hidden intentions.

My uneasiness upsets Dorian, and he turns ever so gently, gazing into the bookshelf beyond the cupboard's glass door. "That's André's level." He slashes a hand in the air as if tracing the specific shelf, the directions lost due to the difference in height between us. "I can't really see anything of it from where I am!"

It is an awkward conversation—volatile and meaningless, hopping between unrelated topics like a petit jeté that doesn't follow any melody—yet the night brightens as he talks, fading away while the clock ticks high above us.

Ever so slowly, the words tumble out of me, like loose, brief questions hazed by the doubts surrounding his true intentions. The clock strikes half midnight when I dare a few sentences. An hour later, we chat about the ballet, the motions, and how to land properly. He chuckles and I giggle, and when he's deeply caught in an anecdote, I listen attentively, captivated by experiences so different to mine.

Dorian leaves moments before the daybreak and I watch him go, repeating some of the words we spoke because my emotions are tucked beneath my music box.

In a few days, this conversation won't mean anything anymore.

The days blur after that, but I keep dancing.

One night, Dorian comes and talks to me, although I occasionally avoid him—I cannot decide whether to like or suspect him. His conversation helps my speech, but it's terrible for my mood.

My envy envelops me, and I yearn to be like him. Perfect. *Unmarred.* Like I was before.

That unstoppable jealousy intertwines with the irony of how my routine—now so dear, now so longed for—felt boring, taking me back to long-forgotten thoughts.

When the sisters repulsed me and I thought they twins didn't belong here... while now I admire their resilience albeit we never spoke another word to each other.

It confuses me. It fills me with misery.

The mornings blend into afternoons and nights and, sometimes, I'm truly looking forward to Dorian's visits. They ignite something—that jealousy, most likely—sorrow, even mild delight... but at least, with him, I *feel*.

I wake again, cushioned by the velvet pillows of my box's sleeping compartment. A yawn overtakes me as I stretch, feeling my arms relax—yet when I raise onto my elbows a ceramic flake remains behind, glaringly misplaced. Picking it up, I roll my shoulders and haul it into another compartment; one bulging with the rest of my debris.

Perhaps I'm only storing them as a reminder of my flaws to one day refute Behati. I am broken, splintering with every hour that passes... but my duty calls me.

Elongating my legs into a few tendus, I begin with a petit battement, timed with Margot's clock. The movement warms my body, the non-existent music blossoming in my imagination— unfolding, growing portentous as I assemblé en avant thrice and across my dance floor.

The boy—when did he arrive?—dashes to my cupboard, unlocking the doors and winding up my box's key—even as I dance. He is alone and doesn't care whether I'll fall, so I plié, balancing myself until the quivering ends, my dance floor stabilising as a new tune surges, this time sonorous and andante.

It roars, rotund and resonant as I leap in a grand jeté, landing elegantly before twirling in as many fouettés as the melody demands. I slow down on its rallentando, and when it purrs to an end, I coupé into an attitude en avant, leg nearly straight, hand poised up to—

Needles puncture my waist, that sharpness shrieking from behind me. The pain shivers through my back, tinkering with my emotions as I rely on my magical mask to offer my gently fractured smile.

My hand endures extended for the boy to touch and, for once, his forefinger approaches me. His smile of half-hooded lids sparks a need—for his approval, his attention, his awe and amazement—and my grin broadens, beaming genuinely with the anticipation his recognition builds on me.

His fingertip grazes mine, ever so slightly and gentle—and slides down to push harshly into my palm.

I stumble out of the pointe but quickly reset myself. My thoughts scream in fear, and terror creeps through my body, but my ~~awful, horrifying~~ smile stays on.

The boy snorts only once, straightening and swiping his long black braids over his shoulders. He locks the cupboard's doors and departs without casting another glance in my direction.

My heart beats faster until the afternoon, even as I struggle through the tendus and stretches, letting dusk fade into the night.

By then, as the shadows engulf me and the other shelves flare alive, Dorian's cobalt gemstone glares at me, pleading, each pulse building the awareness of the need inside me.

Glancing at it, I take a few steps forwards but then retreat, balancing sideways while struggling with myself, indecision swaying me back and forth. I change my mind immediately, twice and again. Once more, and again and again, each time faster than before until I dash towards the compartment, clutching the gem and swiping my hand over it.

It doesn't take long before those known footfalls resonate on this shelf. I pretend to gaze through the glass door, but soon enough, Dorian clears his throat, dipping into a curtsey.

"Are you well? I thought the boy... poked you." It's only a hush, but Dorian sounds half-annoyed. "I saw it with the mirror André gave me."

A sigh escapes me, unruly. What I hear in his voice is *not* concern—he is likely upset because I kept dancing. After all, Dorian was bought to replace me, and his music box now sits where mine once was. He's only concerned about losing the boy's attention... but why did I call him then? Because I needed to be reminded of how pitiful I am? Of the grace I lost? ~~How do I beg him to stay?~~

"I... didn't notice," I whisper at last, feeble just like my lie—but it matters not. My ballet will continue, and my acting will prevail until no magic is left in me.

He frowns, the elven spell smoothing his perfect brows into an impassive look. Perhaps I imagine it, but he scrutinises me with a sprinkle of concern—and I chuckle at that, confused and struggling to scowl, pout, or grimace before surrendering to a vacant, elegant expression.

"I don't want to talk," I mutter, defeated, lowering my gaze and wishing he would stay, nonetheless.

Gently, I look beyond the cupboard's glass door, letting the quietude absorb me—or at least pretend to do so while remaining obnoxiously aware of my surroundings. The other bookcases and cabinets are sparkling to life and brimming with lights, and part of me wishes to be included... or not. I cannot decide, and so that restlessness carries me towards the edge, where I sit with my fractured legs tucked beneath me.

Dorian moves again, his footfalls gentle as he rounds my box, staying on the shelf's floor. He leans against the side—but near my position—glancing beyond without even glimpsing at me over his broad shoulders.

Is that... *respect*? ~~It's mockery; he's ignoring me~~. An offer of company? ~~It's an insult, he mocks me~~. Conflict arises within me, edging between understanding or fighting the idea—but as my thoughts battle each other, the night fades away.

Dorian stays, feet barely shuffling in place and moving after a few hours to stretch before leaning against my box once more.

It is late when he finally steps back, doing a deep révérence, face wrenching as if defying emotions. "Take care, Lyra," he whispers, his hand etched on the music box's gilded rim. "Call me whenever you want."

He departs before I can reply, and I'm left alone, stupefied and mildly outraged.

A new daybreak shines, golden and bronze, the wind ululating through the curtains as I wonder what day it is. I don't remember whether the boy is due to come, and forgetting his routine *terrifies* me.

Weighted by that elusive idea, my stretching requires more effort than it should, but it's not my body that whines—but my thoughts and emotions. They ache, sluggishly seeking to retreat into the comfort of the stillness that only exists between the velvety pillows of my sleeping compartment. ~~Where the boy isn't present.~~

But even like this, embittered and bothered by this ungainly desire, I coil shyly around the dance floor before standing in sur le cou de pied—feet wrapped at the ankle, and ready to leap.

The boy doesn't come today, and although my body aches from holding this position, I breathe relieved.

The room remains quiet during the afternoon, and—for once, like long ago—the need to dance for myself plagues me. It teases me so much I sway in petit battements, practising tendus and easing into splits, all while dust falls from me. A fissure shrieks, a crevice deepens, but it's been so long that I'm accustoming to them. The fractures won't go, I'm faulted and broken, and no amount of magic would fix me.

Even like this, I dance and move. To the clock's tempo or to my own humming, to the noises in the corridor and those on the other levels.

I hop, swirling and arching en derrière, face up and arms extended. My breathing eases as I wait while a fissure sneaks through my countenance, beginning at the corner of my mouth. The magic saves me the embarrassment, keeping a modest feigned smile while my gaze etches on the table ahead—dreading, for a moment, that the boy was back in the room.

A quietude surrounds me. Pounding, heaving with my breathing and calming me into the tiredness of the aftermath—gentle like my soft relevé. I imagine the boy's awed glances from before my first stumble, his loving words of magnificence and mastery, but instead of soothing me, those memories plunge me into a fugue of emotions.

I want to cry, but the tears won't shape. My mouth doesn't grimace but curls up hideously, obnoxiously. *Grinning*. Distressing. So much that—

"I saw you dancing through the sisters' mirror," Dorian. Gentle, standing far away from my music box and averting his gaze for a few heartbeats. He shuffles nervously, glimpsing at my startled figure and blushing. "I t-thought…" He stutters, so unlike himself, before whispering, "I wished to dance with you."

A chuckle burst from me, annoyed by his cruel joke. I never really replied to his signals, instead limiting myself to reaching out of ~~interest~~ duty. His gemstone even sparkled once or twice, calling me... and I never visited his level. Only once, when I tapped it without reigning in my thoughts.

"Lyra..." He whispers, taking a single step forward, his hands kept at his side.

Evidently, Dorian comes only ~~out of worry for me~~ to humiliate me, to toy with me. ~~Because he worries.~~ To goad me. My lips purse, but my brows remain relaxed even when I want to scowl. I lick my ceramic mouth, feeling the chips, prodding the cracks at the corners but unable to understand myself. I struggle with the language and my emotions, wanting to cry and scream, but also sob and pretend he isn't teasing me so cruelly.

"You... don't need a dancing partner," I whisper after a long while, my voice trembling with pain. "Don't tease me with that." Steadier, breathing. Etched on how the moonlight softens my reflection in the dance floor's mirror. Broken; worthless. Fractured beyond sense. "You aren't seeking a dancing partner, but someone to enhance your performance."

Dorian stares, attempting a few sentences but mumbling uselessly. "I'd never—" Stammered. Fidgeting with the strings of his coat. "I don't—*Please*, I..." Pitifully avoiding my stare while his slender fingers massage his forehead, the gesture as polished and smooth as everything he does. "I was honest and meant it. I know you can't see it, but—"

"Don't. *Please*, just don't." My voice thins imperceptibly, and I take a few steps back to hide myself in the shadows—like the first time we met. "Why do you want more attention? The boy *loves* you!" I break, the pain sneaking through me like the ever-expanding fissures traversing my body. "If you came to mock me, just *go*. I don't need you to use me or think you must help me. I'm—"

Broken. Fractured. Falling apart with every breath. ~~Lonely. Afraid. Terrified of losing myself.~~

My voice cracks again, or perchance it's the fracture spanning my neck. "Leave."

"Lyra, please." Dorian takes a few steps en avant, his hand poised so casually it seems unreal and planned. Too polished to be genuine—he mocks me even on this. "Forgive me; I didn't mean it like this."

~~I want to believe him~~. I can't believe him.

"~~Please stay~~. Leave." I repeat, my words fighting my thoughts, juxtaposing my envy of his smooth flawlessness, the loneliness consuming me, and the ~~heartbreak~~ anger of this outcome. "Good night," I manage, summoning my courage because nothing else is left within me.

Silence, echoing like a broken string.

Pain. Rippling like porcelain just shattered.

"Forgive me. But please..." Dorian bows, holding there while his breathing hiccups wildly. "—*please*, know that I meant it. Honestly, I want to dance with you."

He departs after that, and in the ensuing quietude, only his footfalls rumble through—no longer confident but stumbling, rushing while my heart picks into a gallop.

Alone, I slump into the sleeping compartment, hiding the gemstone I was still clutching, a maelstrom of hidden emotions bursting into me like an overture that cannot be ignored—not even as I sob. So mild, so muffled by the velvet, so stifled by the magic.

As the night fades, that overture roars until I cannot ignore it. It takes me a long moment, but I eventually find *it*. That truth somehow hidden within me, muted by my apathy yet sharp and pungent like my misery.

Like my fall into the floor, I fell for Dorian.

For his gentleness, his laughter, and our idle conversations. His respectful caring, his daring approaches, his blindness to see me as someone... valuable. As someone *worthy*. There was peace while we spoke. With him I felt something beyond my pervasive apathy.

It was my mistake.

Falling into that trap. Believing the impossible: that he—so perfect, so polished—could actually care about *me*.

It was all a lie, and I never realised it until now.

I was living in a fantasy, twisting his ~~care and interest~~ mockery and pity into something else. I was wrong. Oh, so wrong.

Daybreak shimmers across the room's golden filigree, reflecting on the polished central table. Its wood absorbs those hues, flickers of white, bronze, and gold strewn about it.

Peering from my sleeping compartment, I let the breeze—warm and soft—strike me with reality, consuming the tears I cannot spend. They weigh on me as I drag myself out of the velvet compartment, hurrying to hide a few more flakes in the drawer of horrors—the boy will come soon, and I must get ready for his visit.

I move ~~with exhaustion~~ deftly, sliding onto the dance floor and beginning my stretches—until, a few tendus after, Dorian's last words crawl back to me. The need to frown and scowl overwhelms me, so appalled I am by his daring ~~care~~ mocking, so flabbergasted by my ~~terrible~~ reaction—but I do not fight the magic, and instead smile broadly while my thoughts consume me.

~~I was mistaken and judged him harshly~~. What he said was cruel, and there is no other truth, no other alternative; it has to be a brutal mocking, otherwise, I would have to ~~admit~~ consider he genuinely cares about me... and that I am deserving of such feelings. Flawless, like Behati ~~believes~~ lied.

Confused, I ease into my splits, and practice all positions until my body is warm and I lean into an attitude allongée—my arms poised in waiting and a leg raised perpendicular to my derrière. I feel powerful like this; capable, adept, and swift like a proper ballerina.

The door creaks ajar when Margot's clock strikes the hour, and the mother and her boy come into the room. The sight relaxes me, and I shiver with excitement when their gazes pour onto the bookshelves and cabinets as if seeking today's entertainment. I know she will visit the sisters (oh, how I envy them!), and—

A voice resonates from outside, bassy and unintelligible, but enough to interrupt that silent conversation between mother and son. Without missing another tempo, the woman dips her head, stately yet apologetic, and departs with elegant haste.

Moments pass in trepidant expectation until the boy clasps his hands on his back, embroidered maroon sleeves shimmering with the room's light. He paces through the room, first glancing at the bookshelf near the closed cabinet, then hurrying past it. He turns to gaze mischievously longingly at the clock above my cupboard but then follows his round, slipping through André's bookcase. A few more tempos pass as he reads the books' spines before he stares at *my* shelf.

I brim with ecstasy when he hurries to *my* level, emerald eyes posed on me while he gently—ever so gently, like that first day— unlocks the glass doors.

The latch clicks open and my heart beats allegro, ignited because he came to *me* without wasting a glance on Dorian. He looms over and I grin joyfully, eager to dance. He holds the box and I ease into a plié, counting the turns of that winding key before the music unfurls, coy but romantic—just like his own smile, so delightful and heartwarming.

Eager to please, I swirl into a fifth position, melting into a balancé and swaying sideways before tiptoeing around the dance floor. I lose myself in the tune, feeling the music vibrating within me just like in those first days upon my arrival. The interest reflecting in the boy's emerald eyes consumes my attention as I return to myself—and dance, free and unrestricted.

I haven't seen him like this in such a long time! Giggling, skipping in joy, and following me with his gaze whenever I leap. He gawks at my grand jeté, smiling in approval at my gentle cabriolés, and nodding gently when I twirl into a final arabesque, my hand reaching for him just as the music slows down to a halt.

Controlling my breathing ~~because everything hurts~~, I stand firm while letting the magic ease me into a delicate smile—yet my heart skips in a ballonné, excited as the boy's forefinger stretches towards me. I approach him, fingers curled as I blush at his smile, so delighted and awed the truth glimmers in his eyes.

The boy liked my performance! I'm still worthy! I'm still valuable!

His fingertip nears, and my hand edges for him, yearning—but he melts into pure spite, eyes narrowing with malice. His forefinger locks behind his thumb's tip, snapping while I watch, thoughtless and confused.

The nail hits me on my chin and my head bobbles back, breaking my posture. I tumble, sight blackened by agony, magic swirling around me. My jaw screeches, and the boy pokes my navel, upsetting my stomach and forcing me to stumble backwards.

My world swirls in tandem with my thoughts, all scattered like the starlight falling from me.

He hurt me; he damaged me. ~~He's angry, distressed~~.

My fractures offended him. ~~It was my fault~~.

I'm worthless, I'm broken. ~~Why am I here?~~

Clumsy and half-blinded, I trudge and bounce against the music box's open lid. The mirror oscillates, ululating loudly and befuddling me with all the sounds cluttering together. The mirror's rippling echoes, my heart pounding in my chest, my ears buzzing, and—

Is that laughter? Is he giggling at my useless balance?

Stumbling forwards, my legs bend as I trudge, undecided between tiptoeing or walking. He laughs when I land on my knees, hands spread to prevent my face from reaching the ground.

Everything hurts.

My knees are numb, my tights tremble, and my hands and fingers are covered in fissures. My jaw aches and I lick my lips, hoping to still have my ~~fractured~~ features in place. Prodding my neck, I tap upwards while following my chin's rough texture. I exhale with difficulty and my cheeks puff, lips curling into a smile—my jaw is still there, and I breathe with relief, mustering my strength.

Rise.

I *must* rise.

Must... do I? Must I dance?

I blink; once, collecting my breathing. I am still alive.

Setting my countenance, I feel the magic coursing through me. Onwards, the ballet will go on, and I will dance while I'm alive.

I feel the pain, the pounding on my body. I wish—

~~Stay down.~~

~~Stay broken.~~

~~Stay—~~

Liar! I am alive! And I *will* dance.

There is no music, just the boy's caustic giggles and the bouncing mirror. I raise inelegantly, mouth parted and heaving, landing in first position, heels together and toes pointed out. I lift my arms into a fifth, arched and barely grazing, just enough for the stardust to fall over me.

Then, I dance.

My petit battement develops into a grand before decanting into a sideways waltz. It is a challenge, my defiance, just enough to catch the boy's attention. My changement mutes his laughter, standing in fifth position, hopping and shifting feet until I move en avant.

Rounding the area, I lean in an arabesque on each corner, grateful to the dance floor that didn't break alongside me. My stardust keeps falling, and there are flakes on the ground, but my smile reflects too lovingly chipped and splintered. A brisé then, coiling towards the centre and revealing a grand adage.

I offer him my cracked forefinger, again and always. It's my defiance, so subtle but consistent, now and forever. Whatever happens, I will go on dancing, enduring, albeit my heart pounds in my chest and I have nothing left to lose.

The boy scowls at my gesture, his eyebrows knitting together while I shiver in fear. My shoulders shake and I stand with trembling legs, gaze fixed on him, the clock's ticking finally resuming.

Moments pass until the boy retreats, slamming the cupboard's doors and stomping out of the room without glancing back.

I ease myself, arms falling to my sides, eyes closed not to look at my reflection.

Pain is a mild word, too limited to convey my current self.

Ache. Agony. Strain. Spasms.

The cramps in my tights, the swirls inside me, the edges of my vision blurring into blackness. The air is thin and sharp, and my breathing is jagged and rough.

My thoughts are empty as well. There is nothing but brokenness within me. A vacuum. Apathy.

I look at my cracked fingers and cannot care.

My chipped face beams back from the reflection, but it's hollow. My pointe flats are fissured, but I don't mind. All of *me* is marked, marred, and mangled, but I cannot muster the strength to care.

I ease myself onto the dance floor and use my hands to help me stretch both legs, holding to my feet to elongate my spine.

The ceramic stops shrieking after a while, and I lay down on my back, needing to rest.

Slowly, lazily, I drift off into nothingness.

A rumble purrs towards me, constant and distant. Margot's clock tickles somewhere above, rhythmical like a metronome. For a moment, I think Behati is speaking her soothing words of pretty lies.

There is something more. Perhaps a hand touching my chin, a gasp that sounds too much like Dorian's.

What day is it? How long has it been?

The pain is still here, and the darkness seems real.

I am... *exhausted.* Sleepy and weary. I do not wish to rehearse today, just to sleep.

I groan, pained, and that tenor comforts me again. Maybe, I shall pretend it is Dorian's and doze off to the sound of his humming.

Dusk filters purple and amethyst into the room, casting a surreal glow on the surrounding furniture.

How long has it been? What day is it?

My lids are heavy but they open sluggishly to look into the shelf's right side, now illuminated silver by the moonlight. There is a golden glow, and after concentrating, I can hear a baritone humming and muttering.

Is that André? It sounds like him, but not; similar but different.

Closing my eyes, I feel my breathing, prodding the many

sensations tingling in my body—then turn to lie on my right shoulder, arm extended, while watching my fuzzy reflection in the floor's mirror. It is scattered with ceramic flakes and chips, but my arm has the same cracks as before.

Pleased that my limbs are still with me, I curl to watch my hands, noticing the fissures and the rough spots where the ceramic's glazing has chipped beyond repair. I rub my fingertips, feeling the grainy texture, before caressing my mouth—whole, with the fractures in the corners and the chips near the chin. Moving down, I prod my jaw, grazing the edges and trying to move it while dust spills through.

There is a new dent just below my chin, shaped as a ~~nail~~ crescent moon.

That voice from before rumbles again, and I finally notice a light coming from far away on the shelf. It calls to me, gleaming so homely and cosy I'm already imagining a roombox assembled like a lounge, stately decorated, and scented to sandalwood.

My thoughts encourage me and I press both hands into the floor's mirror to raise into a kneel, gaze etched in the distance. Rising is a slow, cumbersome process trimmed with screeches, gasps, and mutters—but the light enthralls me and so I crawl through the music box's staircase, sitting on each step and sliding to the next one until my feet grace the floor.

From there, I trudge clumsily through the shelf because each footfall flares needles into the small of my back.

Yet I must go on. That voice sounds familiar.

Walk. Walk onwards. Always onwards.

There is nothing else to do, no other option except to lie down—I refuse to be broken. Instead, I tumble with each step, seeking the light because my darkness already consumes me with nothingness. It doesn't matter what lays under that light, as I'll take anything but the penumbra I live on.

If I stumble and crack to my demise, I will do so on my own accord.

If I flake away, I will do so while dancing.

Not now; not like *this*.

Wading through the shelf takes an eternity, and part of me seeks the entrance Dorian employs to move between levels... although I very well know I'm moving in the opposite direction. A grim smile curls my lips at that thought—truth be told, I'm not certain *where* that entrance is.

Eventually, I stumble into a somewhat familiar nook, placed between cloth-bounded books, and unlike whatever I imagined.

It is another doll-sized library, but lacking a window and filled with books on its three walls. Two ladders connect with the shelves at different levels, and the light comes from tiny lanterns arranged in strategic positions. Their light is warm, gold and gentle; it feels welcoming, charming, brimming with sage under-standing.

A figurine sits on a red-cushioned reading chair, a thick book spread open between his hands. He is carved from ebony and wearing narrow, gold-made spectacles nearing the tip of his broad nose, copious lips pursed into a dot of concentration. He resembles André but not quite so, and instead dresses in a formal, silk-made outfit hidden under an open black gown with yellow stripes on its wide sleeves.

"Is that... a f-formal regalia?" The question stumbles out of me, as dazzled by pain as I feel.

The ebony-made figurine scrunches his nose to lift the spec-tacles dripping from his nose's bridge. "Indeed, mademoiselle." His baritone is calm and collected, less exuberant and more didactic than André's. "Unlike my brother, I am an educated man."

I tilt my head, confused and still hazed by pain. "What are... were you reading?" My hand clasps the archway's frame and I exhale with difficulty; standing is beginning to feel like a titanic task. "Your b-book... looks d-difficult."

"Observant," he answers, closing it and looking at me from

above his spectacles. "It is a treaty on the Elven Wars of Ierlei. But worry not, mademoiselle, and do come in."

I stutter, half-confused and not expecting his manners. Concentrating is laborious, and so my gaze wanders into the finely carved wood, taking in the minuscule golden details—yet my thoughts, and my appreciation for this place, can barely take form, subdued by my pain and confusion.

"I am Professeur Gérard," the baritone states after a while, his tone gentler than his countenance. Placing his closed book on the nearest table, he stands and walks towards me, proffering his hand. "Would you like to sit?"

He's taller than me, cleaner, more dignified, and exuding knowledge. I try to offer him a smile, but cannot be sure of what my face gestures.

"I'm... Lyra, monsieur," I wince, bracing my stomach while accepting his proffered hand. "Ap-pologies for... arriving unannounced, and p-pleased to meet you."

A pained sigh escapes me, but he catches me deftly, gently curling a protective arm around my shoulders. His wood is warmer than my ceramic, and he guides me to the nearest chair.

"I believe you met my brother, André," he comments casually, assisting me once we reach it.

"André helped me. He... was r-resourceful," I stutter, bending slowly and catching the armrests with both hands—my arms are still strong, and they help me ease into the seat.

Once I'm seated, the cushiony, crimson velvet embraces my derrière and back—blissful and comfortable, so heavenly cosy I have to blink a few times not to doze off. Le Professeur grants me a moment of privacy, roaming through his library to fetch a stool and bring it closer. The journey is short-lived but, in the meantime, my legs throb mercilessly.

Assessing them, I notice my fissured romantic dress is bending correctly to accommodate the chair's shape—likely guided by magic. It may be a minor detail, but it pleases me deeply.

"Other figures come to me for knowledge, ma chérie," Le Professeur says, arranging on his stool. He sits elegantly, pushing his gown to the side and crossing his legs. "So, pardon my boldness, but what do you seek?"

His statement takes me aback, and I batter my eyelashes in hopes a few questions will drop on me. Days ago—or was it weeks? Or months?—I was so full of doubts I could have engaged him in conversation for days on end, while now...

I stay quiet, thoughtless, empty. Devoid of anything and even of pain; it is a fact, something that exists within me but not a feeling. A state, perhaps, part of myself just like the fragments of ceramic that compose me. The only feeling is apathy and nothing else.

The silence stretches like an unending fermata, and although Le Professeur awaits patiently, a modicum of uneasiness builds inside me—how rude I am, arriving unannounced, usurping his favoured chair, dirtying his carpeted floor with ceramic flakes, and remaining quiet when he speaks. My eyes wander about, finally settling on the history book he was reading before I interrupted.

"If you could... w-would you keep reading?" I beckon to the surrounding books, then to the ladders appended to the walls. The nook is filled with volumes from floor to ceiling, and Le Professeur's thick glasses indicate he reads avidly—just like I once danced avidly. "For all your existence, would you read?"

Perhaps my question is not about reading at all.

He chuckles, his modulated baritone souring for a fraction of a tempo. "That's a double-edged question, petite ballerina, and the answer isn't straightforward," he massages his temples, the ebony shushing with the motion. "Every activity has a limit, even those we enjoy. Moreover, they may change over time because, as Sougo-dono says, life marks and changes us." Le

Professeur softens, and he leans forwards with elbows on knees, hands interwoven. "Today, my response is positive, and I will gladly read for all my existence... but two moons ago, it would've been different. Like so, my answer will likely differ after I finish a few more books."

I press my lips, again glancing at the leather-bound book on the table. "Do the others come... for answers? Do you find them in the books?"

Le Professeur smiles—a broad, magnificent gesture displaying teeth of ivory. "That is one thing books cannot provide. But experience does, especially when intertwined with that of others."

His answer startles me and I sink deeper into the cushions, their embrace relaxing me enough to allow me to thread my ~~marred~~ fingers over my lap. I gape a few times, parting my lips and testing a few questions but uttering no sounds. It is a fugue, my thoughts, yet the exhaustion that enslaves me mutes the conflict.

Eventually, a question slithers, half-whispered and dubious. "What does... *enough* mean, Professeur?"

I don't know what I'm asking, and slowly roll my hand as if the gesture would shape into the rest of the question—but I wave it away when no words come, exhaling in defeat. In turn, Gérard rests his crossed wrists atop his knee, head tilted pensively.

"It would depend on what you are measuring," he offers at last, his baritone deepening, grave. "If it is ingredients in a recipe or colours in a palette, *enough* has an upper and lower threshold... but it doesn't seem to be what you ask."

"I meant abstract ideas. Feelings," my whisper quivers, and I fidget with the edge of my dress—mildly, just to feel and not to break as I wait for an answer.

How much is enough pain? Or enough misery? *That* is the actual question I cannot voice. Doing so would reveal something

I'm not ready to accept—and I need my façade... or what remains of it.

"Abstract concepts like feelings cannot be truly measured because you must consider both the personal and the moral limits," Le Professeur frowns, assenting to himself. He lifts a forefinger, pointing at it with the other. "Each living being has a different resilience, established by what they overcame and survived; so is the personal threshold. Nevertheless—" A second finger stretches. "—it does not mean they should be pushed there simply because they can withstand it. That is the *moral* limit, and defining the balance between both is a task without end, ballerina."

"But..." The words halt abruptly, dangling like a misshapen soubresaut that couldn't be. "How—?" Another attempt, another botched movement; a pas de chat more akin to ungainly stumbles than elegant hopping. "Why—?" I whine at last, unable to even understand my own question.

Yet Gérard seems to know the answer, nodding like an experienced Professeur. "Someone may test those limits for many reasons, mademoiselle. Anger is one of those."

His answer startles me and my hands weave atop my lap, tightening enough for my ceramic to shriek. I think of the boy— his wrenched face, his stomps, his ~~malicious~~ grin, the glimmer in his eyes.

"But-t..." I shiver, rubbing my arms and sinking into the chair's cushions. "W-what is anger, then?"

Professeur Gérard chuckles, amused, eyes twinkling. "You are a philosopher ballerina, then!" Realising my attempt at frowning, he waves a calming hand. "I'm only saying this because your questions are shrewd and sensitive, mademoiselle. You do well in entertaining such thoughts."

I pout, bewildered. "But you haven't answered..."

A tempo passes, the clock bounces above us, and Le

Professeur laughs honestly, so akin to that of a child caught amidst a mischief.

"You are sharp, ma brave dame, so let me attempt to answer your question," he prefaces, drumming his fingers over his wooden knees, a pensive pout on his lips. "Anger is a blend of pain and revenge, sprouting from the subjacent idea that one has been wronged in some way." Le Professeur spreads a hand, tapping the stretched fingers. The noises are melodious albeit his words are not. "Anger blends many other emotions like contempt, resentment, bitterness, loathing, hatred... and manifests in multiple ways, such as violence or profanity. Anger is as rational as a non-weighted icosahedron dice, the one with twenty faces," he clarifies, straightening and pressing both hands into his knees. "Some would argue anger is destructive, both for the self and others, while others posit it is a botched cry for help. But more often than not, untamed anger is uncalled for."

Another silence, not quiet but bursting with doubts, terror rimming some of them, anguish punctuating others.

"The boy... is he angry? He... s-stomped out after I d-danced," I trail off, head tilted while I seek the right words. My speech departs me the more I fluster. "H-he even s-seemed... of-fended," I stutter, unable to control my mouth. "What did I—?" The magic stalls my frown, softening me into a smile. "Do you know... *why*?"

Le Professeur doesn't answer immediately, watching me with savvy eyes. "There are times when not even oneself can understand one's own feelings." His baritone is dismal, bleak and rumbling. "—but I would speculate it is due to his lack of empathy."

My face contorts as I attempt to grimace, perplexed. "Emp-pathy? For *me*?" My whisper is just a gush of air, a faint exhalation. It's been... long since I arrived, and the boy was never predictable except when standing near his mother. "I d-don't... understand."

"Empathy..." He lingers, pensive, tapping his chin. "Empathy allows us to understand someone else's reaction, even in those cases when they act unlike what we would've done." He walks both hands atop his knees, as if symbolising two figurines or elves. "Someone lacking empathy will never be satisfied with anything others do. You see, Lyra..." His hands relax, and he pushes the spectacles up his nose. "—it is said that the scarcity of empathy is the root of all evil. However, such is a discussion we do not have time for. I believe... you should rest."

Stiffening on my seat, I cover my pout, tapping my flaking paint. The ceramic displays a calm countenance, but that lie directly opposes my inner turmoil. Le Professeur Gérard speaks of concepts beyond me, ideas I don't even possess the words required to comprehend.

Did he mean my pain is not enough? Or that there is no such thing as enough? Does that mean I should go on? But what if I can't?

The anger. If it's uncontrollable and unexpected, there would be nothing I could do to quell the boy! Did Gérard, then, imply I'm the cause of the boy's anger? Yet perchance not blameworthy?

His thoughts on empathy are incomprehensible. How can an elf understand a figurine? That boy never danced ballet, and watching it from afar, from his different scale, is not akin to dancing! Is it my fault he can't be empathetic? Or am I the spark igniting the fire but not condemnable at the same time?

Confused, I frown in my imagination while smiling placidly at Le Professeur—even when his eyes seem to understand the emotion hidden under my magical façade.

There is an air of finality to this conversation, and I can only whisper, "Thank-k you, P-Professeur Gérard."

He nods in response, standing and proffering a hand. "Although I appreciate your visit, I also reckon you must be tired, Lyra." Kind, soft, and all too aware of the pain still coursing through me.

I accept his proffered hand, dumbfounded, almost clinging to it as ~~he helps me into~~ a stand. I traipse with my own feet, but he grants me a moment to stabilise myself—then lets me loop my arm around his before walking me back to the nook's entrance.

"Do come back whenever you want; I enjoyed your questions." He smiles as he guides me down the steps and onto the shelf's floor. "Rest well, little philosopher ballerina."

I bow, shallow and slow, the motion dragged into a half plié that is not quite so. Turning, I retrace my ~~stumbles~~ steps through the shelf, and waddle back towards my music box, fuzzily guided by the shimmers of the moonlight. It barely illuminates the room, hazed and blurred as if a cloud had obstructed the moon and the darkness strengthened in their absence.

En avant, albeit not graciously, I advance, wanting to chew my lips but only managing to hum and spill dust.

How am I going to uncover the answers to Le Professeur's questions? How will I—?

A figure moves ahead, flickering back and forth near the silhouette of my music box. I jerk in surprise, a small gasp fluttering out of me as my gaze settles on Dorian—nervous, hands toying with the strings of his military jacket.

"Lyra!" He calls as I approach, stepping towards me but halting a few paces away. "I saw... the boy's attack a few days ago. With the mirror I mentioned, and—" Frowning, he taps his chin while inspecting me unabashedly. "I came every day, but you were asleep for nights, and now I t-thought... you w-weren't..." His voice breaks pitifully, and he sighs. "I'm glad you are here."

Dorian seems anxious and I cannot find a fitting reason. Myself? Is he... concerned about *me*? I chuckle immediately; the idea so preposterous it only belongs in a comedy. I'm too fractured to be lovable and can barely hold myself together to offer him anything of value. What could I give except pain and sorrow? Spilled dust, shrieking crevices, nightly sobs, and limited tendus.

"You mustn't worry. I'm well," I whisper, faint and demure while walking towards ~~him,~~ my box through the most shadowed parts. "Don't waste a night's rest here."

"Lyra... let me help. You are not well." Dorian's voice is but a thread thinner than a string worn out to nothingness.

It startles me to a stop, and I curl a hand over my stomach. My gaze lowers, my mouth parts to shape a few words. ~~"I'm... in pain. Everything hurts, and I'm lonely."~~ My silence stretches as sensations ripple unwarranted through my fractured body ~~(it hurts; my body, my heart)~~, and I offer him a smile aided by the magic.

"Thank you for coming," I manage at last, squaring as much as possible before hiding under the shadows. "Please, leave, Dorian. Don't miss a night's rest on my acc—"

"I don't want to leave," he interrupts me, approaching and halting so restlessly that—for a fleeting, gorgeous moment—I believe his concern is truthful... but then perish the thought. "Let me stay with you. I'm... concerned. I care about you, Lyra."

First comes the silence, blank and startled like an unplanned pause—as if the score of my scant thoughts had vanished in the breeze. Then, laughter overcomes me, a titter at first but growing louder and resonant, hiccuped and broken by tears that cannot fall. Dust falls from me, and a few fissures thicken, ruining my face.

~~I am a source of misery and pain! I am broken beyond reason, and I will damage him!~~ Why can't Dorian understand I can't withstand him? Is he lying again? Or is this the empathy Professeur Gérard mentioned?

"Don't tease me with that." My whisper breaks, my giggles long dead, just like I am. "D-don't..." A few more words, too many thoughts. Too many feelings. "P-please..." All stammered, nonsensical and contradicting like myself. "P-please."

Dorian says nothing, taking a step back and respecting my embarrassed silence with as much dignity as possible. He follows me from afar as I trudge towards the music box's staircases, his stance clearly at the ready to catch me were I to fall—but I pay no mind to him. I need the velvet of my sleeping compartment, the dreamless, exhausted sleep that quells my mind and skips time.

I need... answers. Solutions.

To puzzle together Le Professeur's wisdom. To sort my feelings and inner shadows.

"Lyra, please," Dorian calls ~~(pleads? begs?)~~, intercepting me when I'm already on the dance floor. "Let me stay here. We don't have to talk, just like that night so many weeks ago."

His words freeze me in place, my eyes engraved on my reflection on the floor—smoother, thanks to the gentle moonlight.

~~"Stay with me. I'm alone."~~ No. He doesn't need my pain. I have nothing to offer, and he deserves better than me.

"Please. Just... leave," I hush, beckoning to the shelf's end with an ungraciously stiff motion. "I have nothing to offer you, not even a decent dance. And you—" The words lock in my throat, and not because of my impaired speech. "—*you* were bought to replace me. You don't need me to show the boy you are better." Spite; hatred. All feigned, all performed in hopes he'll find someone better than me. "Please, Dorian. *Leave*."

The quietude is overwhelming, barely illuminated by the twinkles from the other bookcases and cabinets, their racket drifting like distant chimes. I watch the emotions wringing Dorian's face, the pull of his lips battling between grimace and grin.

Sighing and shaking my head, I turn to the sleeping compartment when he catches my hand—pulling me towards him, wrapping an arm around my shoulders, and cradling my flaking updo. His fragrance overwhelms me and I remain motionless, arms still beneath his embrace, my tension dispelled with every tempo that passes. Abstaining is easier than reciprocating, but... for once, and only for once, I allow myself to reciprocate. Placing my quivery hands on his hips, I lean my forehead until it rests on the crook of his neck.

Dorian is taller than me, taut, lean, and safe like nothing else has ever been. Safer than Behati's embrace, or André's company. Safer than my sleeping compartment, and than any apathy I ever felt.

How am I going to forget this? Am I selfish enough to give in and break him while I fracture away?

No, not at all.

But the way he cradles my updo, and the rhythmical steadiness of his breathing... It is—

"I admire you, Lyra," Dorian whispers, his baritone modulated. "I could have never endured suffering like you do. I have neither your courage nor your resilience. I—" A pause, a few unintelligible words. A sigh. "I can't fathom your pain, but I understand that... it may be difficult for you to believe me. I was honest about wanting to dance with you. To hold you, to help you, to—" His voice; it breaks. "Give me a chance. *Please.*"

What am I supposed to say? How can I even think?

I only have questions, even more now than after speaking to Le Professeur. I hold on to his jacket, surrounded by his arms, overwhelmed by his fragrance, and at a loss for words.

"You don't have to answer me now," Dorian murmurs after a long while, cheek pressing against my broken updo before taking a few steps back. My fingertips glide over his arm, and our hands touch for a moment. "Whenever you want, tap the cobalt gemstone, and I will come. Even just to share the silence." He caresses my cheek, covering the fractures and watching me affectionately. "Sleep well, un être cher."

He backtracks until the shadows blur his figure, and only turns to slip between the books.

Slowly, and still dazzled by those words, I pull open my sleeping compartment and ease into it. My breathing is ragged but mellow, easing adagio as his fragrance of sandalwood and paint delivers me into a dreamless sleep.

It doesn't take long for my days to melt into the same routine.

Ballet and stretching. Dancing and elongating. Leap in a jeté and ease into tendus.

The days go by, but when the boy returns to my shelf, it is always with his mother.

Every day I wake up with the same questions, the same struggles. The same contradiction that pushes Dorian away while wishing him closer. The same distressing delight that forces me to dance because there is no *me* without the ballet.

One day begins with a petit battement, waltzing sideways and pirouetting. Is there anything else to do but dance?

On another day, I sway elegantly, humming above the music and dancing to any tune. I want to rest, but the ballet goes on. Why? *Why?*

Or in others I plié first, then changement and advance. What else can I do but dance?

Why would I not dance? Dance I shall! But why dance? Why? Why!?? Why dance alone??

A myriad of questions embrace me when the sun lights the room, the answers evading me just like that curtain avoids the breeze—fluttering, shimmering, casting shapes that are quite so but not *right so.*

The nights are different, and sometimes I tap Dorian's gemstone—and he comes too swiftly, a rhythm to his gait, a nonchalant air. When I don't, he arrives past dusk, tiptoeing gently and approaching carefully.

Some dusks he grins and sits beside me, sharing my silence, and in others he talks about the other statuettes, positing the same awkward questions of Le Professeur Gérard. He speaks of Margot and the clock, brings a book he took from André, or stays quiet while I doze off.

Our conversations pass by, just like the days, but those are the only highlights of my routine.

After a while, our exchanges drift into a myriad of themes— yet we never speak of ballet.

I think... Dorian already surmised the reason. The why.

That why.

The one I couldn't fathom until now.

Long ago, I loved ballet, even if I once foolishly thought it was boring because it had become easy. But now? The ballet is a jail and all that is left of who I once was.

One day or another. One afternoon or another.

All irrelevant because every day varies so minimally that I can't distinguish them.

How could I? It's all so… repetitive.

Survival, that's all there is.

Days or weeks later, daybreak salutes me early. I go round and round again, into that same boring routine of pushing through the day for the chance of another night.

The breeze whistles quietly, the silence pleasant and tender —cultivated, even, as if a muted conversation would be spreading. The window's sheer curtains blow into the inside, the sunrays shimmering with dust; each speck as colourful as a rainbow, swirling in the air as if they waltzed to a tune I cannot hear.

It compels me to move, and as I watch that flow from my dance floor, I sway into petit battements not to be idle. It's noon when I hum a few times, closing that melody, and beginning my stretches.

Later, as the sunset wanes and dusk fades into moonlight, I peer at the gemstone and grace it with my fingertips. Only at night I am alive—when talking to Dorian or simply sharing my silence with him.

He arrives soon after, handsome but gentle, offering me an elegant bow before perching on the edge of my music box—and the night hops between anecdotes.

I tell him of the few places I visited, and he shares stories from Le Professeur's books. We sit close together, and even if I prefer the shadowed side, his eyes linger on me. I have no strength to doubt him, no reason to second-guess him... even when I know Dorian can't really admire me.

Dawn arrives again, unrelenting on my fractures, my stardust, my crevices. I endure it only because it's just the interlude before the night.

Before Dorian.

I'm already on my dance floor when the room's door bounces open—too early, oh too early—and the boy dashes towards my cupboard.

He struggles with the doors, shaking the entire armoire just like his braids twist and contort behind him. Horror saturates me as I lower into first position to withstand the quivering furniture, a grimace cavorting on his features when he pulls again. I plié and steady myself, watching him wrench—but the door doesn't budge.

The boy stomps out of the room after many failed attempts, fists clenched while my heart hammers out of me.

Its tempo is unrelenting, just like the ticking of Margot's clock, each beat consuming my thoughts until there is nothing else but the echoes of my fear.

"The boy was rough today," Dorian whispers, rounding on the music box and looking up at me. "Are you well?"

I blink, too stunned to speak, too bewildered to understand. Did the day flicker by already? So prestissimo I didn't even notice? I'm still clutching my chest when I nod, averting my gaze away from his.

It's that consideration I cannot fathom, that ~~loving~~ foolish concern that flares in his eyes.

We don't exchange any words and simply sit on the dance floor together, fingertips grazing, eyes lost in the tiny candlelight flickering on the other shelves.

I yawn, relaxing, and yawn again to wake up when the clock strikes another hour. My cheek leans against Dorian's shoulder, and a blush overtakes me as realisation settles in. What if I scratched him? I study him with nervous distress, but he waves my fear away.

When he leaves, there is a spring to his gait.

I'm settling in fifth position when the room's door creaks ajar and the elven mother slides inside. She glides silently onwards, her cobalt, velvety dress shimmering with the dawn's golden light. Her magic opens the cupboard without touching the lock, and after speaking to the sisters, she comes to me.

The elf is gentle, and barely touches the winding key of my box. It turns on its own, buzzing as it goes, and the music unfurls freely. I dance to it, catching her azure eyes and her rouged smile as I finish in a gentile révérence.

A tempo flickers by, and as the mother extends her hand towards me, the corners of my vision darken with fear. My heart pounds out of me, frantic and—

A caress, tender and affable, benign and tame. Her fingertip grazes my updo, sliding to my cheek as if cuddling it. Her smile is all I can see.

"You are lovely, Lyra, more now than before. Splendid and sublime." Her voice. So, so earnest.

The doors close with her magic, and minutes later, I'm still gasping, half-panicked and half-astonished, letting the afternoon blur in confusion.

What am I to do with that? How could she... say that?

~~Why would she lie?~~ What if it is true?

"Lyra?" Dorian. Again.

I yelp and retreat a few steps, panting and wondering—just like always, it would seem—where the afternoon went.

Worry coats his features for a moment, but then mellows into shyness. "The sisters translated the mother's words for me. They always hear her, regardless of who she talks to," he explains, fiddling with his jacket as I haven't seen him do in a long time. "Lyra..." My name, so hesitant, so affectionate. He dares one step, whispering, "You are perfect, Lyra. Sublime, and I—"

"Don't say that!" I gasp, hands clanking against my fractured face. His words terrorise me, and my heart gallops without sense or direction. "Don't. *Please.*" My voice quivers and so do I, retreating.

I fell for him like I fell to the floor. Unstoppable, relentless, and inexorable—and the more we talked, the more I caved. For that gentleness, that calmness, that non-judgemental quietude. For who he is, and who I am with him. I—

I can't reciprocate his feelings. I damaged him simply by leaning on his shoulders. What could I offer him except pain and misery?

"I have nothing to offer..." The murmur flees me, regret soaring immediately while wishing to give in and embrace him.

"How can you offer nothing when you are everything to me?" Dorian's tenor thickens, passionate. "I hope you... feel the same."

"That doesn't matter," I mutter, nervously pacing the dance floor, all elegance gone least I cave in. "I seldom ask you anything! You visit me and waste your resting time!"

~~I don't deserve him; I would just bring him heartache~~.

I'm such a liar, such a liar.

"What of the nights you listened to me raving about books?" Dorian stretches a finger, counting and gesturing just like Gérard does. "Or when you patiently heard me complaining about the sisters' endless gossiping?" Another finger, another step towards me. "You even read with me that book from Le Professeur! And the other André lent me! We shared the silence when either of us was too gloomy to speak!" Dorian finds my gaze, shaking his head because his face will not gesture. "Lyra, you forget everything you do for me because your heartache feels safer than daring."

I gawk, immobilised. How can I respond? What could I say? I can't *risk* him; I'm not good enough for him!

Dorian sighs, his expression fighting against the magic. "But even if I... c-care for you, Lyra, I can't go on like this." Misery. So much anguish darkening his voice. "I will come again in three nights, and we will talk... perhaps for the last time."

He leaves after bowing, and my night scurries away amidst waking nightmares.

I care about Dorian; more than I ever thought I could. I push through the mornings and afternoons to see him, and that fondness doesn't allow me to burden him... with myself.

The morning blurs with the breeze and the sunlight while I stand on my dance floor, so alone and thoughtful I cannot even twirl into a soft relevé. The noon hops me into the afternoon, and dusk finally brings the gloominess I feel. It is night when I sit near the box's rim, legs dangling on the staircase, thoughts blank like an unused sheet.

A brutish, chaotic thump resonates from afar, and I jolt to a stand, a hand clutched to my chest. Is Dorian here already? Did the days flicker by so quickly?

Cursory words bounce from the shelf's end, and after a few whooshes and shushes, footsteps echo in an approaching cadence. They are not Dorian's; I understand that immediately— yet they are familiar, nonetheless.

Recognising that cheerful pace, I hurry down the staircase of my music box, rounding around it just when André halts a few paces away from me. His tie is flipped over his shoulders, his spectacles are crooked, two of his pockets are upturned, and his hands clutch the lapels of his jacket. He pulls once, rearranging the garment.

"Ma brave dame," he states, a touch of reproach sliding just like his thick spectacles. He pushes them up his broad nose, tongue clicking. "I see talking to my awful, insensitive philosopher of a brother has confused you."

I blink, tilting my head and clasping my hands near my waist —and then peer over his shoulder, trying to peer whether a new ladder connects his bookshelf to this cupboard.

"How... are you here?" I whisper, bewildered both by his arrival and the fatherly concern in his voice. "Why?" A single question, yet it carries so many meanings.

"How? Through the magical bridge!" He waves a hand to the bookcase as if the presence of such a bridge would be common knowledge, then shakes his head at me. "Why? Because you're about to commit a terrible mistake, mademoiselle! You are letting your fear take the choice away from you!"

My lips part in surprise, my features contorting into a grimace of despair before settling in that magic-enforced smile. I lower my gaze, threading my fingers and wondering whether—

"Before you think of it, Dorian didn't call me!" André sounds outraged, stomping towards me while pushing his spectacles up; they slide off again, irreverent. "I came because of you, ma brave dame! *You!* Not the danseur! You *must* accept that other figurines, some as refined as myself, care about you!" Exhaling in frustration, André pinches his nose, speaking more calmly. "You must also accept your own feelings. If you reciprocate Dorian's, you should—"

"I have nothing of value to offer him." The words tumble out of me, as inelegant and unwanted as my traipsing. I meet his gaze, sulking and brooding albeit my face remains stilled by the magic. "I will only... cause him pain."

Truthfully, I care too much about Dorian to let him make this mistake, and so the silence extends even around André. He stares at me, brows knitted under his ever-sliding spectacles, the spirals softening a gesture that would otherwise be soured with concern. I offer him a smile, one aided by the magic, yet his frown tightens when one of my fissures creaks.

He sighs, lowering his head and removing his spectacles while methodically cleaning the glasses with his colourful tie. The silk shushes sibilantly, consuming the time as André clearly thinks before speaking.

"Ah, belle dame, love isn't flawless..." He exhales at last, replacing his spectacles; his frown has eased, and his ebony wood shimmers under the moonlight. "Love transcends the hardships of life and endures past them. Even we, statuettes, are not immutable. Sougo-chan is right; life isn't gentle, and love?" He lingers, a smile tugging at his lips while he glances at the closed cabinet where Behati lives. "Love grows and evolves into affection for every version of you. True love goes beyond fractures, worn-out strings, or dulled eyes." He chuckles, tapping the rim of his spectacles before pocketing his hands. "As I said, do not let fear choose for you, and don't force a choice on Dorian either. Promise me, mademoiselle."

I can't answer him immediately, instead dipping my head to hide my confusion. "You are kind and wise," I linger, glancing to the distant point where Dorian's entrance must be. "I'll... think it through. Thank you."

André hums, not attempting to move. He doesn't seem convinced by my answer, instead staring at Behati's cabinet—but the clock strikes again and he shakes his head.

"You better think through it." His ultimatum remains serious for a moment, but then he laughs, patting his elaborate suit. "I must go, but promise me that... that you won't disparage yourself. You are as worthy of love as any of us."

He leaves shortly after, and I'm left with an emptiness worse than before.

I'm plagued by my emotions, all disarranged and lost, each following a choreography unbeknownst to all others and even myself. I want to run away, to hide from Dorian, but also to run towards him and follow André's advice—yet something stalls me.

The next day is as empty as the one before, and the morning vanishes as I repeat the same stretches, barely managing to plié a couple of times. The afternoon is more of the same, yet when dusk fades away and the night arrives, lanterns dot the other cabinets and cupboards.

I watch them, if only for a moment, wondering whether—

The shelf *creaks*, the wood protesting and shirring—a metallic, clockwork-like screech. Taking the box's staircases, I descend to the shelf's floor just when a magical portal opens on my wooden ceiling.

It swirls azure, streaks of cerulean magic scattering about, the clatter of a clock clamouring from inside. A speck of copper shimmers briefly and a gear plunges down, ricocheting on the floor and spinning on itself. It is tangled with copper hair, and spins about before startling and rolling towards me with bewitched precision. Bouncing on my pointe flats, it retreats a few inches before coiling again and settling, the hairs scattered like the legs of an exhausted spider.

Intrigued, I kneel close by, bending to one side and the other to inspect the strange contraption. It is similar to the pieces Margot hurls without care, and as I glance up, I realise the magic portal twirls clockwise, just like the one in her box.

"Margot?" I murmur, fingertips brushing the gear's centre.

"You silly ballerina!" Her soprano screeches, high-pitched and irrefutable, the gear puffing and sparking. "What did I say about refusing help? You—!" She wails like a discordant violin, and the clock above the cupboard whines loudly. It echoes inside the shelf, the gear near me scintillating. "There is more to existence than the task you were crafted for, Lyra! You won't be less of a ballerina for accepting help, and neither will *Dorian* use you to be more!"

I gape, speechless and muted because I cannot answer; my concerns are too many, too deep, too hurtful to be spoken out loud. The elven boy never focused his anger on Dorian but on me, but what... if my nearness hurts him? What if the boy unleashes his wrath on Dorian simply because he's with me? This isn't just about letting him choose; I am protecting him.

That truth hurts me and I choke on my own sobbing, fingers prodding my cheeks but feeling no tears. I'm smiling, *always* smiling. Even when my heart is more fractured than my body, the only thing my face does is smile.

"Your silence says everything, Lyra." The gear quivers with Margot's soprano, now calmed and attuned to my sorrow. "Life isn't static, chère. Yesterday the clock broke, and I couldn't fit a gear through the portal, and today I'm, ah—!"

A mechanism whines again and the device's hairs twitch, the magic above me flickering multicolour. It whiffs in relief shortly after, the gear flattening over the shelf as if exhausted.

"—fixing four parts simultaneously. And succeeding!" Margot continues as if nothing would've interrupted her, but sounding calmer. Gentler, and more understanding. "Every day you are a different *you*, Lyra. Your time in this room hasn't been easy, chère, but you survived! And you are worthy both regardless of it *and* because of it!"

"But I'm..." Shame tinkles on my shoulders and I close my eyes, not daring to touch the gear not to upset it. "—I'm not myself anymore," I confess, the words so tiny they are almost inaudible. "I don't know who I am."

"Yourself," Margot states matter-of-factly, the gear reddening as if boiling from the inside. "But you won't realise that until you accept that, now, you are a more resilient *you*. You cannot expect to live life and remain unchanged, just like a song will change in every play. Don't—"

The clock above us whines loudly, strings wailing and yowling. I flinch, shocked by Margot's words and whatever is happening, relaxing when the ticking resumes as if nothing would've ever impeded it. Margot sighs, the gear casting her voice floating upwards.

"Don't commit my mistakes, dear one," she adds, her soprano gentler than ever as the gear quivers airborne. "Don't shun away from the help that comes your way and, above all, oser vivre, chère. Dare to live."

Colours burst from it, rainbows of magic arching to each side. It careens in the air, tracing pathways I cannot see, drawing filigrees and spiralling higher. True starlight rains on me when the gear collides with the portal, and as it pours majestically, a black-coated figure appears paces away from me.

"Professeur Gérard?" I ask, bewildered while struggling to stand. "Is it you?"

Dramatically, he rolls his elaborate—and perhaps unneeded—cane with a flourish, pulls the lapels of his regalia, and grimaces. His spectacles remain perfectly in place, held by the sheer will of Gérard's scowl. A long moment flutters by, measured by the clock which now ticks precisely like a metronome, and I curtsey so nonplussed that my ceramic's screeches feel muted.

Le Professeur purses his lips. "Little philosopher ballerina, as my fool brother and Dame Margot said... you are committing a mistake, and I have the evidence of—" Gérard gawks, his speech clearly interrupted by his own thoughts. "I am... I'm..." He grunts loud and frustrated, his flourished cane tapping once against the floor. "I am educated but not eloquent as my brother and, for that, I ask that you focus on the meaning of my words and not on my tone." Le Professeur takes a few more steps, squaring his shoulders and locking his gaze with mine. "You asked me about empathy, and what you are suffering is because of it. Dorian understands you because of his empathy, while you do not comprehend him because of *your own* lack of empathy. You never—"

I gawk, taking a step forward, throat so tight I feel the fissures extending inside of me. The words vanish, unspoken and embarrassed as I lower my gaze towards the floor. Le Professeur is correct, as he always is.

"I never saw the world as he sees it," I whisper at last, unwinding because even though it pains me to accept it, part of me always knew it—just like I always knew the boy's anger wasn't my fault. "Never tried to either."

"Exactly," Le Professeur dips his head, his voice gentler when he whispers, "See the world as he sees it, and you will gain a new perspective, a new experience. You will even..." He halts, stepping closer and placing a gentle hand on my shoulders. "—you may even understand the meaning of *enough*, mademoiselle. This is it. Both for him and for you. Just remember..." Pausing, he licks his lips and exhales. "—remember that you are lovable, Lyra."

Before I can answer, he bows and turns with a flourish, his academic regalia fluttering behind him with each of his steps.

I stay there long after he is gone, clouded by my anxiety,

caged by the feelings I accepted as truthful for so long, and shaken by those I'm only now daring to feel. I move around, fidgeting with my skirt, prodding my miserably broken updo, and practising chipped smiles against my mirrored dance floor because I cannot believe Gérard's last words.

But Dorian will come soon, after the sun wanes again... and the only answer I have is to let my heart guide me.

Steps of porcelain tiptoe near, pacing rhythmical yet undecided, back and forth as my heart races, prestissimo, feverish and unforgiving. I keen to hear with a hand pressed onto my chest, the other extended back.

One, two, a swirl of magic, an exhalation, and finally Dorian's footfalls settle into his gallant gait. Soon enough, I twirl on the dance floor, finding his lovely eyes gazing at me from afar. He seems bleak, approaching my staircase with a dooming rhythm, each step forward as heavy and mournful as the tension between us.

Panicking, I smooth my ruined romantic tutu with my fractured hands, testing a few placements to find the one that hides most of my fissures. My treacherous legs carry me en pointe towards the edge, a thought settling dreadfully amidst the humiliation I feel.

Loneliness is easy to handle, but company is *terrifying*. Dreadful. Enabling the possibility of hurting a loved one, not giving enough, or not *being* enough.

I reach the edge, bowing anxiously and whispering, "I... was waiting for you."

Dorian's features brighten, beaming at me and bowing with a dash of relief and a flare of fear. He steps closer to the lowest step of my staircase and I mimic him, nearing the staircase as we look at each other.

"How are you?" He asks, the sudden honesty in his voice sweeping me like a waterfall that pours into the abyss.

I can't think. I can't breathe.

Suddenly, I have no feelings except the eerie, frightening, and irrevocable urge to run—to my sleeping compartment, to hide from this terror, to find safety.

My breathing rages, my heart springs molto allegro, my body quivers. ~~I should accept the truth; I am broken.~~ I pace back and forth, retreating but returning because there is safety in the compartment but also with him.

"I'm fine, I'm fine." Muttered lies. All lies. **Dare, Lyra!** "I'm... I—" Gasp. Breathe. Clutching my head, holding my thoughts, grounding myself. "I can't go on, Dorian! I don't... I don't have the strength to keep dancing. My calves hurt, and—" I whine, prodding my dry cheeks and stumbling down the staircase, arms extended to reach for Dorian. My sight darkens and I can't see him. "I'll hurt you! I'll only bring you pain!"

His right hand clasps mine—it's cold and smooth, porcelain-made but not fragile, prudent and cautious. *Reliable.* He slides an arm around my shoulders, and I... don't have the strength to move away.

"I know you are in pain, but you won't hurt me. You don't have to dance alone," Dorian murmurs, fingers threading near my nape, tilting my head to press our foreheads together. "I love you too much to let you face this alone." Halcyon, serene. Oh, so soothing, shimmering with a fervour that reaches beyond my fissures. "Let me carry you, Lyra. Let me support you."

"I... want to live, Dorian. *With you.*" The truth spills out of me, uninhibited. Finally unafraid. "I'm fractured and need help to rise again, but when life happens, I'll carry *you.* And we'll—" A sob chokes me, thinning my voice into a whisper. "We'll go on, helping each other."

Dorian smiles, curling a hand on my waist, the other lifting my chin. "You are *not* fractured, Lyra. All of this is you, and I love everything about you." His breathing rags for a moment, and then he steps back, arms stretched but hands still clasped with mine. "Every dance scratches us. Every twirl and every song in our music box leaves a mark on us. But I see them as ornate tokens of everything we endured. Not to be ashamed of, but proud of." Slowly, he traces the chips on my fingers and presses my hand to his cheek. "And you, mon amour, are the most magnificent ballerina I've seen."

I sob, cheeks puffing as I cry paint because the magic restricting my gestures was a lie; in truth, it was only my denial. I laugh because I was scared of living, and Dorian understood me. I hold his hands because this is a promise of a future that was fogged beneath my darkness. And then—finally, *finally*—I speak because the words aren't foreign anymore, and the feelings have names. They always had, but I was too afraid of accepting them, too anxious about what they'll unveil.

"One day... I'll carry you. And another, we will carry each other." I whimper, tears of paint streaking my cheeks and vanishing as I place my hands on his shoulders. "I will do that and more because I love you, Dorian."

He embraces me, and within this peace, a realisation dawns on me.

There is beauty in this room as well—but not for the reasons I once thought. Not because of the gold filigree, the fine porcelain, the gemstones, or the polished woods. This room—this *world*—is beautiful because of the statuettes that live here. Because of their kindness, their knowledge, their experiences and resilience, and their flaws.

Just like them, I *am* beautiful because I'm alive, regardless of the fissures and because of them.

I chuckle at that, for once delighted with myself. "Dance with

J.A. BUVA
2025

me, Dorian," I ask, holding his hand, lost in his eyes and charmed by his smile.

"Always. Together." He traces my jawline, and pressing his porcelain lips into the chip near my mouth. "Here, and in my music box. On the shelves or on the floor. But with you. Always."

That night blends into laughter and joy, and when the dawn's pale light filters into the room, Dorian bows and signals to my box's staircase. I clasp his hand, delighted, and climb en pointe towards the dance floor, advancing in a brisé just to tease him. He follows, approaching after a révérence.

I stand in fifth position, leg straight en derrière, arms poised, front and back. Dorian rounds on me, imitating my legs and protectively bracing my shoulders.

Later that morning, the room's door creaks ajar, and the elven woman slips in quietly, closing behind her. Her azure gown flutters as she glides towards the bookcase, leaning forth and offering André a new set of spectacles. From there, she opens the cupboard with her will alone, and spends a few tempos with the sisters, before startling at us.

Her surprise vanishes immediately, and she studies us with an overjoyed smile, finally leaning to wind up our box.

"Finally," she whispers as a melody unfurls. "You deserved love."

Then, we dance along with the music.

Together. Always together.

Encore Librement!

Author's Notes

Thank you so much for your interest in the novelised version of Dance With Me. But most of all, thank you for your interest in the Author's Notes.

As you know, this is a story about emotional and physical abuse, told through several allegories—and I wanted to 'let you in' on some of the thoughts and ideas that went into creating this story. Although I adapted it from the original book-with-choices (also known as interactive fiction) released on Unearthed Stories, these Author's Notes are exclusive to this edition.

ABOUT THE MAIN ALLEGORY

I have always been quite an imaginative person, always using metaphors to explain things to others—especially those related to emotions. Because of that, and for too many years before writing Dance With Me, I felt like a ceramic doll crafted for a single purpose and broken by life... yet with an insatiable need to go on because, as the song says, *the show must go on*.

That's exactly how Lyra came to be, and why I created this world as it is. Truth be told, I wrote Dance With Me to cope.

Trauma changes who a person is, breaking them until shattering every facet... it chips away who you are until, one day, you realise that there is little left of who you were before. Therefore, Lyra's fractures represent the impact of trauma but also mildly refer to ageing; her fissures are a physical manifestation of the 'scars' many events in our lives will leave on us.

Taking that into consideration, Lyra's initial dislike for the other statuettes (especially the twin sisters!) is caused by her lack of life experiences. After all, Lyra was literally born on the first line of the book, and so she has the emotional maturity of a child. Her meanness at the start is, in other words, a lack of empathy caused by incomprehension. Thus, the more Lyra suffers, the more she understands the other figurines—and at some point, begins chiding herself for not comprehending the sisters.

However, living in an emotionally abusive situation—as Lyra unfortunately does—can make someone hold tightly to the only sense of normalcy they feel they have left. This is where Lyra's focus on dancing comes in. She defined her whole life around the ballet, and thus held into it because it was the only remnant of her life *before* the abuse, short as it may have been.

ABOUT LYRA'S TOXICITY

Lyra is extremely toxic towards herself. Her resilience and obsession with high performing can be easily confused for a laudable effort when, in reality, it is a toxic trait. It is a way to cope, a child-like solution to the abuse she's enduring. Perhaps, Lyra unknowingly thinks, if she keeps dancing the boy will not be abusive.

Has it ever happened to you? Interacting with a person who seems *just fine* and then finding out they were struggling with depression as the result of trauma? Well, it happens. *A lot.* High-functioning anxiety and depression are a thing, and neither is precisely healthy. It is a coping mechanism, and one incredibly hard to overcome.

But where does the trauma come from? Obviously, from the boy's violence... but also from his inconsistency. We all learn in a very straightforward way—do one thing, get a reward; do another, get punished.

Lyra cannot do that. There is no pattern to the boy's behaviour, and that means she cannot find the action that will prevent him from leashing out. Throughout the story it seems that the boy's action have no reason to be... and they don't, from Lyra's point of view. After all, she is the narrator, and one incredibly biased.

But ultimately, the boy's reasons matter not. The abuse is real, the pain he causes is real, and Lyra's fractures are as well. We don't need to understand *why* he does something to gauge the consequences of his actions.

Something else derived from this high-functioning depression is Lyra's limited facial gestures.

On the one hand, as Gérard mentions (in Chapter 7), people without empathy cannot deal with others' negative emotions, especially when they are the cause of those negative feelings. Thus, Lyra is magically (*cough* trauma coping *cough*) forced to smile. In many cases, that happy façade is necessary to remain safe; in others, it prevents people from reaching out because revealing the truth can be dangerous, threatening, or even feared.

On the other hand, and as seen in Chapter 8, the magic spell limiting Lyra's facial expressions was just her denial of her own pain. In other words, there was no spell at all. Something similar happens with Lyra's speech; she couldn't speak because she didn't dare to express (or accept!) her emotions. So when Lyra breaks towards the end (still in Chapter 8) and musters the courage to reveal her struggles, she realises that she'd never had to learn to speak... just to embrace and admit her emotions.

All of this blends to create something else. A detail that posed the greatest challenge when novelising the interactive version of Dance With Me—the strike-through text.

Often, trauma and depression won't let a person see that

there is another path ahead, effectively forcing them to stay on the same track. Sometimes, and in those cases, the alternative feels so outrageous that even considering it is impossible. I conveyed that impossibility with the ~~strike through~~ style. It represents everything that depression tries to override; those thoughts and emotions are known and felt but immediately rejected after thinking about them.

Depression and trauma—especially when ongoing—take agency away, and the fear of what could happen if the abuse ends (it could be better, or it could be far, far worse) may keep the person trapped in the darkness.

ABOUT THE SECONDARY CHARACTERS

But what about the other figurines? Let me confess something: they all say what I needed to hear. In different ways, with different personalities... but with the kindness I craved.

Finally, there is another subtlety in Chapter 8. The boy couldn't open the cupboard because the mother locked it with magic. This is why she opens it without touching the door's lock. Lyra doesn't realise this, so her limited (and biased!) narrator makes no comments, leaving this entire situation for the reader to understand. The elven mother's action conveys that, more often than not, someone has to step in to stop the abuse.

Don't ever be the boy; be the mother. Depression lurks near all of us. Seek help if you need it, and whatever you do, stay safe.

FINALLY...

Thank you. For your interest in Dance With Me, and in these Author's Notes. I struggled when writing them, unsure of how much to share. Just as it happened to Lyra, being vulnerable is *terrifying*.

That said, and as we say in my home country, I wish you success.

~ Livia

141

To Those Who Helped

I am deeply thankful to everyone involved in this novella, both in its original interactive format, and in this novelised edition.

To my partner in life and developmental editor, Fernando. Nothing would be the same without you; you are incredibly supportive, you give me hope, you give me courage. Even when we were starting that dream of us, called Unearthed Stories, you put up all of you to help me shape my vision for this novella. No language is enough to convey how grateful I am.

To Varsha (from Reading by the Rainy Mountain, and Speculative Speculations), and author Joshua Walker—the first two people who read Dance With Me in its interactive version, and supported the story with reviews and blurbs. It meant the world to me, and it gave me the courage to continue. *Thank you.*

To every single blogger, booktuber, author, and reviewer who heeded my call when I asked for support . In no particular order: Holly Tinsley, Tim Hardie, P.L. Stuart, B.S.H. Garcia, Thomas J. Devens, Jarrod Courtemanche, D.B. Rook, Karl Forshaw, C.B. Lansdell, Callum Lott, Jamedi, Esmay Rosalyne, Abel Montero, Zara Y, Kayla, Chris, Indyman, Kristen Shaffer, Kris, and many more. You were fundamental on helping me gain momentum.

To Alison Phoenix, for giving voice to Lyra in the most perfect way ever. For all the dedication you put into nailing all my literary elements. It was a pleasure working with you.

To Jose Arturo Bustamante, for his incredible illustrations that gave life to Lyra and my cast.

ABOUT LIVIA

Livia J. Elliot writes literary and philosophical fantasy, with an emphasis on character development and meaningful themes—especially struggle, control, identity, self-perception, and bias. She's currently releasing two series: *Records of the Orders* (eldritch horror meets political intrigue fantasy) and *Tales of the Bookshelves* (dark, psychological fairy tale standalones). She is also the lead writer of *Unearthed Stories*, an app publishing interactive fantasy and sci-fi for adult readers. On the side, Livia also hosts the podcast Books Undone, featuring literary analyses of speculative fiction.

If you loved *Dance With Me* and want to learn more about the universe, receive exclusive sneak peeks and behind the scenes, and news of upcoming releases, then **sign up for Livia's newsletter** using the QR code below, or filling the form at https://livia jelliot.com/newsletter

www.ingramcontent.com/pod-product-compliance
Lightning Source LLC
Chambersburg PA
CBHW070513170726
48291CB00008B/2736